CW01079767

THE GIRL IN THE WOODS

SUZ KORB

DEDICATION

For my daughters, carrying on my legacy. And our ancestors who went before, all the way back to the primordial soup of life and evolution since.

CONTENTS

"Thus, from the war of nature, from famine and death, the most exalted object which we are capable of conceiving, namely, the production of the higher animals, directly follows. There is grandeur in this view of life, with its several powers, having been originally breathed into a few forms or into one; and that, whilst this planet has gone cycling on according to the fixed law of gravity, from so simple a beginning endless forms most beautiful and most wonderful have been, and are being, evolved."

– Charles Darwin, *The Origin of Species*

CHAPTER ONE

I'm shaking. My body quivers. Sweat beads on my skin. I feel wet with cold and my breathing is shallow.

This room is clean. Too clean. The smell of disinfectant assaults my brain through flaring nostrils. My eyes are wide open, staring at the computer monitor. I'm lying on a hospital bed on top of a thin layer of tissue paper as a sheet. My nerves jangle internally as the doctor moves the ultrasound wand through the thick gel that's smeared over my abdomen.

There are many doctors present today.

For a routine pregnancy scan normally such a procedure is carried out by a sonographer. Not today though. This day is different. This moment is different.

"There is a foetus present." The doctors talk

amongst themselves, not even deigning to consider my feelings. To them I'm just a live specimen on a medical slab waiting to be probed. I bet every one of these doctors wishes they could open me up and dissect me right now.

My eyes dart right and left around the room. This can't be happening. For months I've shown no hormonal signs of pregnancy.

Someone new enters the room, not surprising as doctors are in and out of here all morning. Although, this new someone has the silhouette of a strangely shaped face. I can't see *anyone's* face properly in this darkened hospital room, apart from the doctor's profile that's lit from the soft glow of the ultrasound machine monitor.

"What do I do?" My voice is shaky. I feel light headed, almost as though I'm about to pass out from anxiety. My eyelids feel heavy and all sound of whispered voices blips out.

One silhouette falls, followed by another until everyone in the room is on the floor, except for the newcomer with an odd face.

I'm so sleepy. Won't someone tell me what's happening to my body? To the bodies? Why are they lying down?

The last person standing steps into the dim light of the screen. Not an odd face. No face. A face covered by a gas mask.

"Why am I pregnant?" I ask the faceless one.

"You're not…"

A pause.

"You're not… pregnant, Michelle. Just relax. Everything is going to be okay." Her mask-muffled female reply. The kindest voice I've heard all day.

"I can't be pregnant." My voice chokes on a sob and I know I will sleep soon. "I haven't had sex in two years. I'm... I'm not wanted... this can't be..."

"Sleep, Michelle." She puts a warm hand on my shoulder. "You're going to be okay."

I'm comforted by her soothing voice and words.

I sleep.

.

CHAPTER TWO

There are things seeping into my consciousness. Flashes of light. Streaming sound like wind. I feel a slight breeze on my face. I'm cooled on a surface level, but under my skin I'm hot.

My thoughts are heated.

"Is she awake?"

That female voice. Soothing. Caring. Worried even.

"She's coming to."

Another female voice, this one not as kind. Younger sounding. Snippy, even with just those few words caught in my ear.

Blink.

The sparkling light. It's coming from the sun dissipated between blurred trees that streak by.

I'm in a car. A big comfortable car. My forehead is pressed up against the hard cool window. The vehicle rocks and sways over bumps in the road. It doesn't jolt and jar my teeth like when I drive my beat up little Ford Ka around town.

No, this is a very nice ride indeed. It's large, like a cruise ship on the land.

A Range Rover. I'm sure of it. From this side of the window I know it has darkly tinted glass. The sunlight streams into my face from this end, bright and sure.

"Where am I?" I'm too weak to do anything but speak. I can't even muster up energy to worry.

"You're safe, Michelle."

The kind voice.

"I'm Georgina and that's Elizabeth next to you."

Glancing to the right I see the woman Georgina is talking about. A young blonde girl with a short bob hairstyle. She can't even be out of her teens yet. Though she *seems* old in the way her forehead is creased in a pinched line between her brows.

Why so much frowning for one so young?

I can only see Georgina's profile. She's driving. She looks decidedly older. Maybe in her late thirties.

Not that such an age is old in comparison to how I feel. Her hair is shoulder length like mine, but the similarities end there. My hair is dark brown whereas this Georgina woman's hair is as blonde as Elizabeth's.

I'm old. I feel it in my 39 year aged bones. I shouldn't be feeling this old yet. Should I?

Let out a breath of air. Tired of holding it in. Tired of life. Just want to sleep.

My chin tilts down. My abdomen is in view. My swollen abdomen. A pregnant belly. Something living inside me.

I shriek in terror, causing Georgina to swerve the Range Rover. We're on a narrow country lane and I don't know what happens next because all I see is glass and trees flying past my vision.

CHAPTER THREE

Awaking. Cold. Pain.

My eyelids flutter open. Dappled sunlight penetrates my vision. Grass under my head and hands. I'm sticking out the window of an overturned vehicle. My big stomach feels sore.

Groaning in agony, I pull myself from the wreckage.

There are two women trapped inside. I don't know them. There is blood. Are they dead?

"What's happening?" I grab my pounding head and crawl away. When I find the strength to stand I'm wobbly on my feet.

The sky spins around me for ages before settling down to a blurry view of rolling hills.

Catching my breath a moan escapes my lips. No wait. It was one of the women. She's moving in the overturned white Range Rover.

I keep my distance. I should probably help, but I don't know them. I can barely remember myself and what I'm doing in this unknown place. I don't know who they are or why we've just been in a terrible accident together.

"Georgina!" The younger blonde girl with blood in her hair. She scrambles free of the wreckage and pulls the other woman out of the driver's seat. I move behind a small hedge, silently out of her line of sight, should she turn round.

Elizabeth makes a call on her phone. The other woman shifts around.

"Where is she?" Georgina is awake, her voice croaks weakly. "We have to stop her before she finds out—"

"Ssshhh." Elizabeth soothes her suffering friend. "She can't have gone far."

My body goes rigid with worry. What was Georgina about to say? They have to stop me? Well I'm not okay with that and I'm definitely not going to stick around to find out whatever secrets they're keeping, especially if it means my life would be in danger with these two.

Turning, I slide down the grassy slope. When I reach the bottom of the incline, I make my way out of the clearing into a copse of trees. I travel for fifteen minutes before I'm sure the women are too injured to follow.

As for injury, I'm feeling sore and I need to sit down. I collapse near the base of a tree. The grass beneath me is soft and thickly dispersed with spongy green moss.

My hand immediately goes to my belly. My swollen belly. The thing that caused me to freak out in the car.

I'm calm now, as much as I can be. I'm pregnant, even though I shouldn't be. Yes that scares me, but being taken from a hospital room by two people who want to kill me is playing on my mind far more.

I don't know where I am, I just know I need to get to water first and foremost. I've never felt so thirsty. I've never gone without drinking when I need to and all this craziness is starting to overwhelm.

There's nothing else for it, I'm going to have to

make a move. I can't just stay here and dehydrate.

Pushing myself up, I lean against the tree for support. My belly is about seven months pregnant in appearance. With my free hand I cradle the underneath of the protruding area beneath my belly button. I had to start buying maternity clothes months ago, so I'm especially grateful I decided to wear loose fitting navy blue maternity yoga pants today. My belly isn't huge yet, but I've never been pregnant before, so it feels enormous to me just slightly sticking out like it is.

My white t-shirt is sticking to the sweat on my back.

Standing fully upright I reach round and when my hand comes away I get a shock.

There's blood on my fingertips.

It's now that the pain sets in. I must have gotten injured back at the car crash. It doesn't feel like I've got glass embedded inside me, but I don't know the extent of the wound I'm suffering from. I really need to find help soon.

Should I find a main road though? Those two

women are bound to be on it eventually. Assuming either one of them can walk and aren't too injured.

I've got to take my chances. I'm wounded, thirsty and pregnant. I don't know if it's a human baby growing inside me, but the lack of energy is plainly clear.

Whatever's incubating in my womb is sapping my energy fast.

CHAPTER FOUR

I never made it to a main road, but I have found a
cottage in the woods. I feel like I've been walking
for miles and miles and this is the first dwelling I've
seen in ages.

Feet crunching over the gravelled driveway, my
tongue feels dry and parched like a sponge long
since fished from the sea. I'm holding my pregnant
belly with one hand. I reach toward the red painted
front door of the cottage, but instead of knocking I
test the handle.

It's open and I stride right in.

Heading straight for the kitchen I down a glass of
water in three great gulps.

I'm still thirsty. So I drink more, and more and
more and more, until I think I've been standing at the
white ceramic basin for a full fifteen minutes just

drinking.

Now my stomach is harder than ever. It's not only filled with the body of a baby in there, but I drank too much water as well.

I sink to the floor, my legs suddenly feeling like heavy liquid.

"Who's here?"

A man's voice. He comes into the kitchen, coughs, and sees me on the floor immediately. His dark hair is cut short. He's wearing a tartan flannel button down shirt, blue jeans, and hiking boots. There's a shadow of dark stubble on his chin.

His eyes go wide and he comes toward me. I don't know what's about to happen and I don't have the energy to fight him off. Should he decide to attack me, I'm doomed.

CHAPTER FIVE

I wasn't attacked by the man. The opposite has happened actually. He's set me on a sofa in the front room after bodily picking me up off the floor of the kitchen. It caused him to cough a lot and I was a bit worried about his ability to carry my weight. I've never been picked up by anyone since I was a child. As an adult woman it's a strange sensation.

The fireplace is slightly smoking upwards, as though he had a fire going earlier in the day. Why he'd be burning wood or coal in the summer, I have no idea. Maybe this particular stranger feels chilled all year round.

"I was in a car accident." I blurt this out before he

can ask me any questions. My hand is permanently placed onto my bulging abdomen, but my other hand goes to my injured back. "I sorry to barge into your home, I was in a car accident—"

"Are you hurt?" The man coughs and looks round to my back. "Wait there."

I don't know where he thinks I'm going to go. I suddenly don't even have the energy to mistrust this guy. And I'm right in my assumptions when he comes back into the room with a first aid kit.

"May I?"

I nod in confirmation that he's allowed to check my back injury. I lean forward and he lifts my t-shirt.

"Thanks for this." I feel really awkward letting a stranger help me, but there's nothing else I can do. I went and water-logged myself into a stupor of lethargy. "If I can just use your phone I'll call a taxi."

"Not a problem, Miss. I'm Colin."

I'm not at all surprised that's his name. He has a distinct Glaswegian accent.

"I'm Michelle. It's nice to meet you, I guess.

Since you're being so nice to someone who's basically broken into your house."

Suddenly I feel out of breath from having spoken just those few words.

"Don't worry about it, please. Your back injury is only a scratch. I've put some disinfectant and a plaster on it. Just sit back and relax."

He's so kind. Maybe I will be able to relax, just for a few minutes…

CHAPTER SIX

"I fell asleep!"

Sitting bolt upright isn't easy with this huge tummy in my way, but I manage to do so in desperation. I don't know how I could have let myself fall asleep like that, and in a strangers house no less.

"It's okay." Colin coughs and gets up from where he was seated in an armchair. "Now that you're awake I'll take you to hospital—"

"No!"

Oops. I shouldn't have shouted like that. It's just, there's no way I want to go anywhere near a hospital, not after what happened this morning. Was it this morning?

"Sorry." I apologise in a calm voice. "I don't want to trouble you. I can just take a taxi to hospital."

I won't really go to hospital once a taxi collects me, but this Colin guy doesn't need to know that.

He looks at me with furrowed brow, like a big question mark is stamped across his face. "I'm afraid that won't be possible, Miss... umm Michele."

Not possible? Why not? I'm starting to worry more than ever now.

"Taxis don't exactly come out this far into the countryside."

I wonder how far he means. I don't want to give away that I don't even know where I am, but I don't think there's any way he doesn't already know that.

"What time is it?" I rub my big belly and then my confused head. "Actually Colin, could you tell me the date please? The exact date."

His eyebrows are now suddenly raised in curiosity. "It's June the fourth and it's 4 o'clock in the afternoon."

Right. Okay. So my visit to hospital was a day ago. That's interesting, and worrying.

Where did those two crazy lady's in the Range Rover bring me to?

"Yeah, that's what I thought." I'm not fooling this guy. He knows I'm out of sorts. I am though, if anything because of the car crash. "I think I will take you up on your offer of taking me to hospital."

Only I'll be sure to make him let me out of his vehicle as soon as we reach the nearest town. Again, I'm definitely not going to any hospital, no how no way.

Bang. Bang. Bang.

Someone crashes their knuckles against the front door of the cottage.

"Is anyone in there? We need help!"

It's them. The two women. It's Georgina and Elizabeth. I recognise one of their voices already.

Colin turns to go with a quiet cough and I jump to my feet. My eyes are wide in concern and I grab his bicep before I know what I'm doing. I shake my head and he immediately knows the fear and desperation I'm holding inside. "Please, don't let them know I'm here."

"I…"

Colin whispers and puts his hand on top of mine.

"I won't. Don't worry."

My big belly relaxes in on itself and I feel safe for just a moment longer. Somehow I trust him. I know Colin will keep the secret of my presence in his home.

He goes to the front door and has a casual chat with the desperate women at his door. When I hear him ask if they need a lift to town I almost panic out right.

Luckily they thank him and get on their way.

When Colin comes back into the room he whispers to me again. "They asked me if I've seen you. Well, they described you. Are you in some sort of trouble?"

*I breathe out a sigh of relieved air. "Not any more, I hope. Thank you, Colin."

His brows are raised again, questioningly.

"They looked injured. Were they in the same car crash as you?"

Oh great. Now starts the questioning. I don't know how much to reveal to this guy. What if my instincts have been incorrect so far? How do I really know I can trust him? Maybe I'll answer a few of his questions, but only for a little while until I can be sure Georgina and that Elizabeth girl have gone far enough away from this cottage. I should take him up on his offer of a lift to hospital as soon as possible. Even though that's not where I'm planning to go at all.

"I… umm… oh gosh." I feign light-headedness. It doesn't take too much pretence on my part. My big stomach has been a growing burden these past few months and I'll take any chance I can to sit myself down. And that's just what I do now. I slump onto the sofa. "Why didn't they take you up on your offer of a lift into town?"

"They said they had help coming, but were worried about their friend. I gather they meant you."

"I'm not their friend. I don't even know those women." I grumble. "I know their names, but that's about it."

Colin looks at me with deep concern, right before he coughs a couple of times. The older woman called Georgina looked at me like that, but she turned out to be a weirdo when she was with that Elizabeth girl. I can't just ignore their strange behaviour. They basically kidnapped me and now I don't know where the hell I am!

"I'll be right back." Colin turns and makes his way into the corridor and the second he does a crack blasts through the glass of the front door.

"Elizabeth, no!"

I hear Georgina scream from outside. I'm on my feet in a flash. Colin grabs my arm and hauls me into the kitchen at the back of the house. My big belly slows me down, but I'm hurrying as fast as I can because that shot that cracked the glass was from a gun.

My breathing is hard. Colin grabs a pack from the back porch area. When he slings it on his back it makes him cough quite a few times. But hurriedly we soon vacate through the kitchen door and enter the back garden. Through the gate his cottage butts up against the thick of the woods. We reach the line of trees and hurry in through the dense foliage.

"What's happening?" Colin hisses. He grabs my

22

hand and pulls me along. It helps me go faster, despite the heavy weight inside my womb. "Why are those crazy women trying to kill you? This is insane!"

He's telling me? I don't know what's happening to my body, let alone why Georgina and Elizabeth seemingly want to kill me because of it. Or maybe that's the problem. It was Georgina behind that gas mask at the hospital. She's the one who took me away from the insensitive doctors. And didn't I hear her scream at Elizabeth after that gun shot went off?

"I don't know what's happening." I can barely speak. I'm running out of breath and my temperature is sky rocketing. "I… need to… stop."

"Just a bit further and then I'll be able to get signal on my phone to call for help." Colin pulls me further along and we come out on the shoreline of a lake. He seems quite out of breath and starts coughing as though it's the only way he'll catch his breath.

"Is this the Lake District?" I gasp, dropping to my knees.

"Yes of course it is. Are you all right?" Colin

supports my arm as I fall onto my backside.

"I'm so hot."

"You are." He touches my forehead that's wet with perspiration. "You're burning up. Your baby might be in danger—"

I don't hear what he says next because blinding white heat envelopes my vision. I cry out but I can't hear my own shouts of agony. I'm writhing on the ground and I start tearing at my clothes. I've got to get them off before I burn up completely.

The lake. It's my only hope of cooling down. The calm waters call to me like a beacon of ice to a smouldering meteor bursting from the sky.

Crawling forward on all fours my belly is big enough to scrape the ground gently as I move. Colin's hands are all over me, he's trying to stop me from getting to the water. He doesn't understand. I have to immerse myself. I don't know why I'm so hot. I don't know why I need to get into the lake so badly, but I do and my life depends on it.

Finding a burst of strength I rise to my feet and kick Colin between his legs. I don't even feel bad about it. I can't. There's nothing I can feel but fire boiling in my veins beneath my skin.

I race towards the water and dive in. I hear splashing behind me and I know Colin is following.

He must not save me from what I have to do.

I know I need to go deep. It's the only way I'll cool down. I trust the lake. It won't kill me. If I dive now the lake will save me.

I do dive. I go deep. I swim down and down until light from above blanks out completely. The only way I know which way is down now is to let out bubbles of air that float up and away behind me. I don't follow the bubbles up, I swim down and away from all light. I reach the bottom of the lake and the water becomes thick with silt. I can't hold my breath any longer. I have to breathe in. My lungs are screaming for oxygen.

I inhale.

Water pours into me. I choke and my spine spasms backwards. Cold water instantly lowers my fever. I feel chilled and no longer hot. My big belly is light in weight under the water that fills me now both within and all around.

The water inside my lungs is like a spherical wall shutting me off from a world of air. But the oxygen I need is there.

I'm not drowning.

I'm breathing underwater.

I'm not going to die down here.

But I'm not going to remain conscious either. I just know that the coming sleep will not be my end. I know this somehow even though it feels like I can't explain it to my own mind.

I will not die at the bottom of this lake. I will only sleep.

CHAPTER SEVEN

The sound of water lapping at the shore. I'm lying on my front and I taste stones near my lips and they taste of wet minerals. My eyelids are closed shut, but light from the sun penetrates making my vision orange. I'm naked and exposed to the outdoors, I sense that much without looking. The pebbles beneath me are starting to dig in and it's making me feel uncomfortable. The air smells fresh and there's pine on the breeze.

My eyes fly open. I can see clearly and I'm up on my feet in an instant. Looking around I find I was right in my assumptions. I'm at a lake. A boat in the distance is sailing closer to my location and I'm suddenly very aware of my nakedness.

I've got to find some clothes right now. I'll worry about finding my identity later. Because that's the biggest problem here.

I don't know who I am.

My memories are foggy. I can't think straight and I don't know how I ended up by this lake. The more I walk though, through the woods, the more I start to remember.

A fever.

I was hot.

So very hot.

I remember the water cooled mc. I'm surprised I don't feel cold right now. I've never walked around outside with nothing on. If someone comes along right now I'm going to be embarrassed beyond belief. But there's nothing else for it. I need someone to be here. I need help and I know it.

More memories. My brain is kicking into gear.

I stumble over a sharp pebble and cry out. "Ouch!"

Hissing through my teeth I grab my foot and sit down on my bare bottom.

Rub my sore foot. Concentrate on remembering. Think, Michelle, think…

That's it!

I know my name.

Of course I know who I am. Memories have flooded back into my head, and with it a lot of blood flows to my foot, soothing the pain.

And then there's the pain of realisation.

My stomach is flat. There's no baby or anything bulging inside me. I'm not pregnant. I wasn't pregnant before. Was I? Before what?

Before I entered the lake.

I swam down into the lake. I know I did. I breathed under water! I slept down there in the dark depths and I awoke mere minutes ago at the lake's edge.

My foot no longer hurts. My head does.

What do these memories mean?

"Colin."

I say his name aloud.

"Georgina." Hers too.

And Elizabeth. She fired a gun at me! At Colin.

"Oh god." I grab my aching head. I'm so confused. My life is a mess of convoluted memories.

My life changed for the worse the day my mother died. And then the growth erupted inside me. The ultrasound showed there was a foetus inside me that day at the hospital. But my hormones showed no signs of a pregnancy. I remember the sonographer saying something about the foetus' cranium and organs, but what it was she said, I can't recall. All I know is that's when Georgina had arrived, wearing that gas mask.

I must go on. I can't stay here out in the open like this. Naked. Vulnerable.

When I get up to go the pain in both feet returns. It's torture walking on the rough ground. I don't know why I didn't notice this before. Probably because I've been in such a state of disarray since waking next to the lake.

This whole day is insane. My life is insane. I'm not familiar with the territory I'm in. If only I had never gone to the hospital that day, I might still be close to home, close to friends. At least I'd be some place where I knew another human being.

Suddenly, I'm aware of something familiar. Sort

of.

It's a cottage. I've been here before, even though it can't be something remembered from childhood holidays in the Lake District.

No, I've been to this cottage recently.

It's Colin's house.

I sink to the grass once again as memories flood my brain. Why is this happening to me? I remember, I forget. My mind is awash with misfiring synapses. At least, that's what it looks like behind my eyelids when I close them shut.

But this is a good thing. I'm sure this is definitely Colin's place.

"Oh no."

Sitting bolt upright I remember more.

The gun shot. That's the reason we fled the cottage.

Is Colin even alive? What happened after I submerged myself under water? Why did I try to drown myself? How am I here right now with a flat stomach and no weird pregnancy inside me?

I need answers and the only way I'm going to find

them is from Colin. If he's even there.

I go in through the back gate and I'm only half way to the door when the man himself opens it.

His face is covered in a thick, but short and trimmed dark beard which I don't remember from mere hours ago. Then again, I've been confused about the days lately. But the man before me is definitely Colin. If I remember anything recent it's the man who helped me. Even if he is still a stranger.

"You. It is you, isn't it?" His face is a picture of surprise. His eyes are wide and roaming over my naked form. "Here, let me…"

His voice fades as he turns away, but only briefly. Soon enough he's wrapped a soft warm blanket around my body and is ushering me gently inside.

"The gun shot!" I cry out, halting my footsteps. My voice seems to collapse and despite the fact I seem to have crawled from a lake of water only moments ago, I'm very thirsty.

"It's okay."

Colin's words are so comforting. I'm not panicked about that Georgina woman or Elizabeth any more. I can't be, my head is still too muddled.

"Let's get you settled down and I'll make some tea."

Yes. Hot tea. That's definitely what I need right now. Something about a high fever crosses my mind, but it's a fleeting memory and I don't linger or dwell on it. I don't want anything to confuse me further and worrying thoughts won't help my situation.

Colin is so kind and I tell him as much. Or I at least try to. "Thank you." I'm grateful to him as he seats me in the front room, a somewhat familiar place, even if I was only here for a short time before...

Before that crazy girl Elizabeth...

Oh my head. I can't deal with this memory problem. It's like my brain is scrambled egg and its constantly trying to un-cook itself.

I'm lying horizontally on the sofa while Colin goes back into the kitchen, so I lean my head back against the arm of the couch.

Just relax and don't think about anything.

Words inside my mind are thoughts, but I'll try

anything to get my brain to be quiet for just a few minutes. I need to calm down if I'm ever going to be able to make sense of things.

"Here you go." Colin hands me a steaming mug of tea.

I take a sip and the sugary milkiness warms my insides.

"I didn't ask how you take it because I figured you could use quite a bit of sugar right about now."

He's not wrong there, and his conversational tone helps to ease my mind. I'm feeling much calmer now.

"I'm sorry about all this." I hold the cup in my hands, warming my palms and fingers on the hot ceramic surface. "My life is…"

What? My life is insane. That's what it is. But it's more than just completely crazy and I don't know how to put it into words.

"Some things happened while you were gone, Michelle."

I look up into Colin's eyes as he speaks. He coughs a few times. He's sitting at an angle to me in an armchair, his own cup of tea in hand. I have a feeling he knows something about me, and I'm not quite sure I want to find out what that something is.

A huge yawn escapes my lips.

"But maybe we'll talk later. You need rest." Colin stands and coughs. He sets down his tea and ushers me upstairs.

I sit on the edge of his bed where I finish my tea. It's so good going down I even drink the dregs. I think Colin is saying something to me, but I'm too tired to mentally process his words. I look at him though, standing there in his tartan flannel shirt, dark jeans, and hiking boots. He's so real. So in charge of all his faculties. He didn't question my appearance on his back doorstep much, and right now I'm grateful for his description and calm demeanour. I need a steady person in my life, if only to bring balance to my chaotic thoughts from the outside.

Staring at my bare feet I can't stop the drowsiness from consuming me. I let myself fall back onto the fluffy duvet. I think Colin tucks me properly into bed, but I don't know for sure because I fall asleep immediately.

CHAPTER EIGHT

It's nice to wake in a warm bed, and even nicer having a clear mind. I wake well rested and not at all confused about my identity. I don't even remember dreaming, but that's a good thing considering the fact that I probably had nightmares of drowning that I wouldn't want to recall anyway.

"Colin."

I say his name aloud when he enters the bedroom, and I'm now acutely aware that my voice sounds strange to my own ears.

"Them." Clearing my throat I sit up in bed. "I'm sorry, I don't know what's wrong with my throat."

"It's a different throat."

What a strange thing for him to say.

I look at him as he brings in a tray of tea and toast.

"Sort of." He adds. Setting the tray over me. "I'm

sorry, I shouldn't have said that."

Despite the fact that I'm thinking more clearly this morning, I'm starting to get confused all over again, and it's not by my own doing. I don't know this man, but I've experienced quite shocking things with him in the few hours I've been in his presence, all together. Maybe he's always like this. Perhaps he always talks in riddles and he likes for people to figure him out. Although, I get the feeling he's the sort of person who doesn't normally like the company of people at all. Not if I'm judging by his secluded place of abode, away from crowded society.

The entire time I've been contemplating his demeanour, I've also been eating. I've scoffed toast and I'm pouring a second cup of tea when he speaks again.

"We need to talk, Michelle." Colin sits at the foot of the bed. "Georgina and Elizabeth are down stairs and—"

He doesn't get to finish his sentence. I fling the tray aside. It crashes to the floor, dishes cracking and breaking everywhere. I roll off the bed on the opposite side to Colin. In a split second I notice I'm wearing women's clothing that fits me well. Too well. How did I come to be dressed? And where did the clothes come from?

There's a large window behind me and it's standing wide open. I crawl through it before I have time to think upon my actions.

"Michelle!" Colin leaps around the bed and comes after me.

I'm already out and stepping down across the low roof of the floor below. I wouldn't have been able to do this if my belly was still swollen to the size of a woman in late term pregnancy, but I feel more agile now than I have in years. My body is fully energised and capable. I fling myself easily down the side of the house and I'm off and running in my bare feet. I know I'm not going to get far like this, so I push my way into a thick growth of shrubs and hedge where I wait.

Soon enough Colin comes charging past and he's not alone. That Georgina woman and Elizabeth are with him, only neither women look the same. I remember Elizabeth having a short blonde bob and now her hair is down to her shoulders in length. Georgina's hair looks more silver than blonde, even if it's the same length as I remember it.

Who are these people? What's happening to me that I should suddenly become a victim of these strangers?

Once they've all passed out of sight I try to relax, but I'm in a state of shock. I don't notice I'm playing with my hair until I look at it clenched between my fingertips.

It's my hair, only it's different somehow. The same brown shade, but the ends look like they've never been cut and the length is a bit shorter than when I went into the lake.

Everything about me is different since going into that lake.

I take a moment to stare at the back of my hands. Everyone thinks they know the backs of their hands. But honestly I guess I'm just not the type of person to notice how often I see the backs of my hands.

What I'm seeing now though, doesn't look like my hands. At least, not the hands I've known for many years.

My skin is soft and pale. I have two freckles on the back of my left hand that are still there, but there's something missing.

There are no scars.

Besides being in hospital recently for my strange pregnancy, I was hospitalised for appendicitis as a teenager. I'd had an I.V. badly inserted into my vein that left me with a large scar from knuckle, nearly to my wrist.

That scar is gone. And so are the others. I check my body everywhere I can manage to twist and turn in this shrubby cramped space.

The scar on my right knee cap from when I tripped and fell as a child chasing after my new kitten. It's gone.

Another childhood accident where I'd crawled up shelves in my friend's storage room and the whole thing came crashing down. At the time my right leg caught a large nail that was protruding from a plank.

That scar is gone too.

"What happened to me?"

Maybe the question is *what did Colin let Georgina and Elizabeth do to me?* Did they scour my body with some kind of dermabrasion laser? If they did, *why* did they?

My mind is awhirl with unanswered questions. Perhaps I should just let them find me. I have a feeling they are the ones with the answers I need. But there's just no way I'm going to trust them. Elizabeth shot a gun at me. Colin must have been in league with them all along.

I don't know what I've stumbled into, or what kind of messed up people I'm dealing with. I think they've gone off far enough in search of me now. I'm going to have to risk going back to Colin's cottage. At least for some shoes. After that if I can find my way back to the lake I nearly drowned in, I'm sure I can find someone on a boat to help me. I'll swim to the nearest dock if I have to.

Treading carefully and as quietly as I can I come out of the hedge. I find my way quickly back to

Colin's cabin. In through the back door and he's got some green wellies there that I slip my feet into. They're too big, but they'll do. They might flop a bit loose on my feet, but at least the ground won't tear up my bare soles instead.

I spot a backpack nearby and fill it with bits and bobs that are close at hand.

The front door opens.

Damn. I took too long!

Racing through the open back door I don't have time to quietly shut it behind me. They'll know I was here. If I hurry though, they won't know when I was here and they might figure it's too late to catch me up now.

"Michelle."

I halt in my tracks.

It's Georgina and she's blocking my escape route through the gate.

"Get away from me." Adrenaline has kicked in, shooting my heart into super-fast beat mode. If I don't expel this nervous energy soon, my shaking hands will go numb.

"You have to talk to us, Michelle." Georgina splays her hands. She's dressed like someone who's going for a long hike, so I know she came prepared to deal with me in her own ways.

Well I for one, don't plan on sticking around to find out what those ways are.

"Michelle."

I turn half way around.

Colin and Elizabeth are standing in the doorway of his cottage. Well, Elizabeth is behind him, hear arms folded in front of her. She looks as though she wants to step away from me entirely.

"Leave me alone!" I shout and run towards Georgina. I aim to push past the woman but she pulls a gun out of some pocket, halting my footsteps.

"I don't want to use this!" She yells. "Please, Michelle, you must have questions about your body. We can answer those questions if you'll only cooperate."

More adrenaline surges through my veins. I feel like I'm going to explode in frustration and fear.

"Just get out of my way!"

Zshoop.

A near silent shot rings out from the gun. I'm hit with a bullet in my shoulder and I cry out. But my voice catches in my throat. I go down like a lump and everything whites out like pale nothingness before my eyes.

CHAPTER NINE

Amazingly, I'm not dead and like this morning when I wake I have no doubts about who I am. Where I am is another matter.

I'm back in hospital and I think I'm here because Georgina shot me.

The first thing I do when I sit up in the hospital bed is to check my left shoulder.

It's not bandaged. I wasn't shot. Wait. I was shot with something. There's a red dot the size of a needle point on my irritated skin.

"Please don't freak out again, Michelle. You're making us first time rejuves look extremely immature."

Elizabeth is standing in the open door way and she's dressed like a doctor, which doesn't suit her at all considering the fact that I know she's too young to hold any sort of medical degree.

I don't know what she's talking about and if her and Georgina are so anxious to explain things to me, this is hardly a civilised way of going about it.

"I was shot." I look Elizabeth dead in the eye. "I know I was shot."

"Yes, you were. With a tranquilliser gun."

Wonderful. So now I'm being treated like an animal who's got loose from the zoo. Add that to the way I keep getting treated at hospital and I'm really starting to feel like a guinea pig being experimented on.

"What hospital is this?" I demand of Elizabeth.

"It's not an NHS hospital, that's for certain." She laughs. This blonde sneering bitch actually snorts at me.

I've never actually punched anyone. I've talked about doing so online, who hasn't? But I've never wanted to bring physical harm to anyone until now.

The least this girl deserves is a slap.

"I'm guessing your parents never taught you any manners. Hang on... is Georgina your mother?"

"No."

She has to be. I'm sure of it. "What kind of mother teaches their child to shoot people? If you were my kid you'd be grounded for life. Now please do fuck off. Shouldn't you be in school anyway?"

Elizabeth's reaction is more scoffing. She smirks and snorts a laugh again. "Only if you go back to secondary school as well, Michelle. I'd say you could do with proper A-Levels a second time around."

I'm about to launch myself out of bed and have at this brat of a girl, when she comes at me instead. I sit up straighter and Elizabeth snatches something off the bedside table. She presses a button on the remote in her hand and aims it at the wall. I watch as a panel moves aside to reveal a very large floor to ceiling mirror. It's faced directly at my bed, or is it? The person lying there isn't me.

Is it a window into the next room?

I can't help but stare and stare at the girl on the hospital bed.

Just staring and staring and not wanting to notice the other person in that room.

It's Elizabeth. She's not standing in another room. That is a mirror I'm looking at, not a window. Elizabeth is standing next to the girl on the bed in the reflection and the reflection is me, only I'm no longer age thirty-nine at all. I look no older than nineteen.

My mouth opens in astonishment. I'm at a loss for words. I don't realise it but I've already slipped out of the bed and I'm slowly walking towards the mirror. The hospital gown I'm wearing is open at the front and I stare at my half naked reflection.

"I'm... I'm..."

What am I? How can this be happening?

"You're young again." Elizabeth sets the remote down and crosses her arms. "If you want to know how it is that you're youthful, I suggest you don't run off like you keep doing."

I hate to admit it to myself, but she's right. I need

answers if I'm ever going to make sense of what's happened to me. That doesn't mean I have to get my answers from her though. "Why are you here?" I talk, but my eyes don't move from the mirror until I do up my hospital gown. "Why are you speaking to me? Where's Georgina?"

Not that I want to speak to her either, she's the one who didn't miss when she shot at me.

In my bare feet I head towards the door.

"I said don't go running off again!" Elizabeth is trying to tell me what to do.

Opening the door I'm met with a visual that takes me aback for a moment. This definitely isn't a normal hospital, and it's certainly not an NHS hospital. I don't think an NHS hospital would have the budget for a building like this.

The walls are all glass. I can see out into the woods. It's like a panorama picture all the way around, everywhere I turn down corridors as I hurry along.

"Michelle." Elizabeth is following me. "Where do you think you're going? You don't know your way around here."

I pass doctors in scrubs, some of them wearing long white lab coats as well. There's something strange about the doctors though and it's the fact that so far everyone I've seen is a woman.

There are no men here.

"Is this building circular?"

I don't know why I asked that of Elizabeth. I can tell I'm going around in a big circle. Still, all I see outside are trees and more trees. I haven't even spotted a car park out there. No roads or even dirt trails lead up to the other side of these big windows. What's also very off-putting is the fact that I haven't yet found a door, be it glass or otherwise.

"Where's the exit?" I demand of Elizabeth, finally halting in my steps. When she snorts in response I realise I'm back at my hospital room. "Where can I get some normal clothes?"

Finally, I get an answer. Maybe not in the form of words, but Elizabeth goes to a tall cupboard and opens it. I rudely push her aside and take stock. Scrubs, underclothes and lab coats are inside, along with a pair of very comfortable looking walking shoes.

"What about the clothes I came here in?"

Again, Elizabeth keeps silent.

Fine. I don't need her to say anything. I just grab the clothes and shoes and shut myself in the bathroom. After I'm dressed I look like a doctor with the lab coat on, but it's not like there was a cardigan in that cupboard to keep me warm. I'm guessing they don't really want me running off again, if I do manage to find the exit. I'm not going anywhere until I find out what's happening to my body, but after I do I'm definitely out of here. I get the feeling that even though this place isn't a public hospital, I'll be treated like a lab rat nonetheless.

When I leave the bathroom I find Elizabeth is gone.

Good.

I'm not in the mood for anymore of her scoffing in my face.

I go to the door and find the handle is locked. I'm about to fly into a rage about that, but then it turns and opens from the outside.

It's Georgina who's opened it.

I barge past her into the outer hall. "Please show me the way out."

"I will, Michelle."

She will? Well that was easy.

"After we've explained some things."

"Show me the exit now and then you can explain anything you like."

Georgina rubs her forehead as though frustrated, but before she did I caught her eyes glance at the wall of windows.

So there is a way out through the glass, I just need to find it because I don't think I'll be let out of here as easily as she's making it seem.

"Come with me."

I follow Georgina half way around the circular building. We stop at a chrome panel in the central wall. She puts her face up to a built-in scanner, the likes of which I've seen a lot of, but only in movies. The thing beeps and the chrome wall panel slides open to the side.

It's an elevator. We both step inside and when the door closes my stomach leaps into my throat almost immediately.

We're going down and at a very rapid pace.

Finally our descent ends and the metal door slides open to reveal a long concrete corridor lit from beneath lights sunk into the edge of the ceiling. We step off the lift and walk down the length of the hall to a set of double chrome doors at the end. Again Georgina's face is scanned before the doors open. We go through a hatch that blasts us with warm air.

"Hyperbaric chamber." Georgina answers my unasked question.

The door in front of us opens and we walk into a vast room the likes of which overwhelms my senses.

I'm rooted to the spot. I can't move for what I'm seeing. I can't take all of this in. What am I looking at here?

Floating bodies. I'm seeing bodies in tanks of water. One body per square tank.

"What is this?" I shriek in horror. My eyes are watering with the death I'm seeing all around me. I round on Georgina. "What are you doing to those bodies?"

She backs slightly away, but not before I've grabbed her arm. She's wearing the same clothes as me and the white lab coat fabric crumples under my grasp.

"Michelle."

Someone's said my name, causing me to release Georgina and whip round.

A group of women are standing by the large glass vats. The vats that contain the bodies of women too. Everyone is female in this place, even the dead ones.

One of the doctors steps forward. Her black hair is pulled up into a bun so tight I'm wondering if she can even blink. "You've certainly caused a lot of trouble, young lady."

Is she talking to me? She's looking at me and yes I know I look young now, but my mind is nearly forty years old. Besides, she's one to talk. She looks about the same age as Elizabeth, not even out of her teens yet.

All of them do. Every woman standing there

doesn't look like a woman at all. They all appear to be no older than high school age at most.

"Why are you speaking to me like that?" I approach BunHair. "Who do you think you are, little miss?"

She smiles a little and it makes me again want to punch another human being in the face. Her face. Her smug know-it-all young little face.

Instead of lashing out though, I put my face in my hands. I don't know what's come over me and I can't concentrate while seeing the floating bodies. I'm so angry at everything. Even my fear is translating as anger. And I'm definitely afraid. I'm afraid of this place because I don't know what any of it means.

"Walk with me, Michelle."

The girl knows my name. Of course she does.

"Who are you?" I take my hands away from my eyes and I can already see she's walking away between the rows of big vats.

"I'm doctor Hathor, but please, call me Bernice."

How very chatty of her, as though we're just taking a friendly stroll along a park trail in the city.

A far cry from where we actually are; a place far from reality if I thought I was dreaming.

"Okay, Bernice. Why are you harvesting the bodies of dead women?" Might as well get straight to the point.

"They're not dead, Michelle." She looks up at a glass vat filled to the top with water. In it floats a naked woman. A pregnant naked woman. They're all pregnant. Each body that floats in its own tank is in varied stages of pregnancy and the further back along the rows we walk, the further along I notice the pregnancies are.

"They're alive?" I keep walking, staring at the tanks.

"As alive as you and me."

"What's happening to them? What are you doing to them?" I'm feeling frantic. Something's not right. Each woman is further along in pregnancy than I've ever seen before and now some of them are starting to look like they're carrying sextuplets. How can any woman be this pregnant? The further down the rows I go, the larger the stomachs of the women get.

"This is impossible." My eyes are wide with inner terror.

"This is what your body went through in the lake, Michelle."

What is this doctor talking about? How did I get to be an experiment like this?

"We haven't done anything to these women other than to provide them with a safe place to be reborn."

Now what's she saying? I can't mentally process her words.

"What the?"

I've reached a tank with an impossibly pregnant woman inside. Her belly is huge and it extends and wraps around her middle. She's floating in that water with her eyes closed as though she's blissfully unaware of the shape her body is in.

"This can't be." I'm losing it. I have to know. I hurry along faster from one tank to the next, each woman now more grotesquely deformed than the last. "What's happening to these ones?" I cry out, backing away from the vats now, but for some reason I've gotten turned around. I'm still heading deeper into the rows of tanks. The horrors I'm looking at make my mind want to pull away, but my eyes won't close. I just keep looking and looking at the sleeping floating women that don't even look human any more.

I stop at a vat and stare at the form within. "They aren't pregnant, are they?"

"No. They've each grown their own clones within their bodies. A new body for themselves, if you will. A younger body."

Doctor Bernice Hathor goes on to explain things to me in very clinical terms.

"Do you see the large protruding deformation behind her skull there, Michelle? That's where her brain has started its descent. It will travel down her back along her spine over the next few days. Then her brain will install itself into the cranium of the new body within her womb. Once the brain is intact in the new body, the old body dissolves as nutrients for the final stages before awakening. She will no longer be nearing the age of forty, she will be nearing only twenty once again."

I'm finally able to look away from the tank and I'm now staring —incredulous— at the young looking doctor. But she isn't young, is she? She's like one of the women in these tanks.

She's got a new younger body that she grew within her.

"Is that what happened to me?" I swallow, hard. I know what her answer will be, but for some reason I don't think I'm ready to accept it just yet. So instead of waiting to hear what she's got to say, I make a run for it.

The doctor doesn't follow me. I dash around vats and tanks, each one with a floating deformity inside it. When I've almost run out of breath I realise the women in the tanks are now young girls. These must be the one's who's old bodies have already dissolved. So they'll wake up at the age of almost twenty, rather than forty. Which means every woman here, even the ones who looked young above ground in the hospital area, were all at least forty years old in mind, if not in body.

I've stopped running to think.

If my body can do this by age forty, then what will happen when I near the age of forty again? Do I get another clone inside my womb? Do I get second chance at second chance at renewed lifetimes? Will I ever die?

Maybe it wasn't such a great idea to run off like I did. Now I'm going to have to return to Doctor Bernice's presence —or whatever her name is— and ask to find out more.

Or do I want to know more?

Yes. I have to know because the thought of living forever scares me like nothing I've ever felt before.

CHAPTER TEN

I don't know how long I've been sitting at the base of the tank full of water, but something brings me back to reality in the form of loud beeping.

The tank I'm leaning against is emptying out of water. I don't know where the water is going, probably some pipe under the tank, but the level is lowering and with it the body of the girl inside is sinking to the bottom.

When the tank is emptied the girl is left lying on the grated surface at the bottom of the container.

I'm on my feet, my hands and nose pressed to the glass while I stare in.

She lies there, her dark wet hair plastered to the

fresh young skin of her face and neck. Clear liquid drains from her nostrils and slightly opened mouth. When I look up from her lips I notice her eyes are open.

She's looking directly at me. Her irises are as black as her pupils and I feel as though if I were to shine a light in there I'd see straight into her forty year old brain.

Suddenly she starts choking and coughing, spewing the last of the water that must have been sitting in her lungs after the draining.

When she's breathing she rolls over and lies flat on her back, knees bent and pointed upwards. Her hands go to her tummy where they feel around. I'm guessing she's making sure she doesn't look like she's fifty months pregnant any more.

The doctor approaches with other women in tow. The ones I saw with her upon first entering this insane laboratory. Because that's what this compound still is, to me. It's a giant lab that doesn't hold sea-life in its tanks, but a species of humanoid women all unto their own.

That's what I am. I'm not human. No human woman can clone herself within herself like this.

Maybe we're all aliens from another planet. I don't know what to think. I'm deeply confused as I watch the women help the newly young girl in the tank.

"Well that was good timing." Elizabeth strides up. "Did you see her wake, Michelle? You could have had an easier time of it if you'd come here instead of trying to drown yourself in the lake."

I'm not really listening to her snide remarks. I watch as a hatch opens in the side of the tank. Two girls enter the vat to help the newly young girl inside. Elizabeth starts talking again and I really don't want to hear what she has to say. I do want answers, but I think I'll talk to Georgina from now on.

Talking of whom, the very woman I'm thinking about comes round one of the vats. She looks oddly at Elizabeth who nods her head.

I'm wondering what their wordless exchange was all about when suddenly Georgina grabs my arm.

"What is this? Payback for when I grabbed you? You have no right—"

Georgina hisses in my ear, quietly. "Please shut up now if you want to live." Loudly, to everyone else, she shouts. "We'd better finish your brain scan to make sure everything's connected and in working order, Michelle."

She moves me by force past the tanks and back out to the elevator. We take the lift up and I'm back in the hospital room within seconds. I'm not about to stay here though. I've never been treated this way in my life. I don't like *not* being in control and having other women order me around. It's doing my head in and I feel the loss of freedom deep under my skin.

Georgina closes the door. "There's a problem. A serious problem." She's wringing her hands and she appears to be very nervous. "Doctor Hathor is doing something very wrong."

"How long have you known her?"

Georgina looks up at me like I'm speaking another language.

I try to clarify. "I just mean you think she's doing

something wrong only now? I could tell that girl wasn't right in the head the moment I laid eyes on her too-tight bun."

Georgina gives a half-hearted laugh. "I like you, Michelle. I really do. I knew I was right to rescue you from that hospital."

I don't exactly consider what she did 'rescuing'. At least I might if I knew more. "So what's the wrong thing Bernice has done?"

"I don't know… that is, I don't have concrete proof of what she's done, or is planning to do."

"Can you give me a hint?"

Finally, I think she gets the point. I'm not going to understand anything she's talking about if she won't tell me. I understand the woman doesn't trust me, but why should I trust anything she says either?

"Doctor Hathor is killing us."

Now we're getting somewhere. "What do you mean?"

Georgina starts pacing back and forth. "I was trying to find out how many times she's rejuvenated—"

"Rejuvenated?"

"How many times Doctor Hathor has been reborn. How old she really is. I was poking around in her office and I saw some plans about not letting rejuves... sorry... not letting us rejuvenate more than five lifetimes." She stops pacing and looks me dead in the eye. "I've lived through five rejuves, Michelle. And I think Doctor Hathor is going to kill me for it."

Five rejuves, or lifetimes? So if we always rejuvenate around age forty, that would make Georgina at least one-hundred and forty years of age. Maybe even older because I think rejuvenating means going back to our teen years.

I look really young. I feel really young and energetic. Younger than twenty, that's for sure.

"Did you find out how old Doctor Hathor is?"

Georgina still looks worried. "I think she's thousands of years old."

I don't say anything. Georgina doesn't say anything. I sit on the bed and stare at the wall. "How do you expect me to believe anything you say?"

"I don't. I really made a mess of your rescue from

hospital, Michelle. I'm sorry. But you've been uncooperative, which is very unusual for women like us."

"What do you mean?" Turning, I face her.

"Your mother was supposed to tell you about your true nature, Michelle."

"You knew my mother?"

She nods and I'm taken aback. "My mum could… she was a…"

"She could rejuvenate, yes. And I think she had been doing so for a very long time before she decided to have you."

I'm getting confused again. There's so much to this rejuve thing that I don't understand.

Georgina notices I'm confused by the look on my face. "We can chose weather or not to be reborn, Michelle. And if we want to live a normal lifetime we can get pregnant for real. If we do become pregnant with a normal foetus before the age of forty, our bodies will not create a clone. We will grow old past the age of forty and most of us die of old age problems, but we also become susceptible to disease and cancers."

This is too much information to take in. It's not as shocking as when I first saw the tanks, but my head is still spinning with all this new knowledge.

"I guess you'd better leave this place then, right?" I'm looking at my young reflection in the mirror now, even though I'm talking to Georgina.

"It's not that easy. Everyone is monitored. We've all got tracking chip implants. Doctor Hathor knows how to find women like us all over the world. That's how we found you, Michelle. Even after your mother died in that car crash a year ago."

Wait. Did she just say a year? "How long was I under the lake?"

"It takes months to rejuvenate, Michelle."

Months. I've missed out on months and months of my life. Not that I won't have another lifetime to make up for it.

Oh this really does my head in thinking about the possibility of *forever*. Or not forever if Georgina is right and Bernice is ending our rejuvenated lives whenever she deems fit.

"I believe you." I say this point blank to Georgina. "If you say Doctor Hathor is thousands of years old, but if you need proof, then I'll get it for you."

"But you don't have security clearance."

"Then you'll have to help me with that, but I want you to know that I'm going to help you too." I'm also going to help myself get the hell out of this place. She said something about an implanted tracking chip. Well that's not going to fly with me. I am my own person and I don't want anyone keeping tabs on my whereabouts on a twenty-four-hour basis. And I certainly don't want to be killed off whenever one girl thinks she's in charge of my existence. Besides, I might decide to have a real baby someday.

"I thought you might help. You're different, Michelle. You didn't have a mother to tell you who you really were. You've dealt with all of this and I can tell you're not one to conform."

"Exactly. I'm not going to live my life... or lives... or whatever... I'm not going to live in this place."

"Oh we don't live here. We just chose to

rejuvenate here."

"So I can live my life wherever I want to?"

"Yes, but you're still tagged like the rest of us."

I hop off the bed. "And therein we have a problem. You said I'm implanted with a tracking chip?"

Georgina nods.

"So how do I remove it?"

"That's not possible. At least not without setting off about a million personalised warnings."

Sighing loudly I open the door. "Show me to Doctor Hathor's office."

Georgina follows me out of the room. "We can't just barge in there, Michelle. This entire compound is a secret and it holds deeper secrets inside. If the rest of the world knew about us... well you experienced a bit of that at hospital, remember?"

Do I ever. I know what she's saying. She's telling me we'd be experimented on. The secret to everlasting life? From what I gather we just evolved this way, but knowing humans (because I am one, thank you very much) men and women worldwide will want a way to tap into the chance to rejuvenate. Something that might be a possibility if scientists ever got the chance to experiment on us.

I'm going round and round the corridor in circles, talking in hushed tones with Georgina. "Does Elizabeth know?"

I get a nod in response.

"Then why is she such a little bitch?"

Georgina stops walking, forcing me to halt as well. "She's a lot more angry with Doctor Hathor than I am."

"Why?"

"Because I'm her mother and I don't think she really wants me to be killed soon."

Right. That makes a bit of sense. "But if you're her mother aren't you going to die of old age?"

"I'm Elizabeth's adoptive mother."

Oh. Right. So Georgina should be rejuvenating soon. I wonder if her clone is growing inside her right now. She's not showing in her tummy area, but she does look as though she could be nearing the age of looking like a forty year old woman, again.

"If you're really up for this I will get you into Bernice's office. But you have to stay in your room for the next twenty-four hours."

My only answer is a nod of the head. I go back into my room to look at my face in the mirror. I never thought I'd see this face again, except for in old photos from when I was at sixth form.

"How did we ever evolve to be like this?" Sliding my hand over my cheek, I'm still watching my reflection when Elizabeth enters the room.

By the look on her face I'm guessing she's spoken to Georgina about my participation in certain matters.

"If you fuck this up, you're dead."

I don't know how to respond to that. My eyes start to water with indignation. Why is this girl always so beyond perturbed?

"What is your problem with me?"

Elizabeth kicks the nearby waste bin. It goes flying into the far wall. "Georgina is my mother."

I haven't moved from my place in front of the mirror. "She's not your real mother though. Let me guess, you're birth mother was able to rejuvenate, but after she gave birth to you with your charming personality, she became a crack whore—"

Elizabeth leaves, slamming the door shut after her.

I'm surprised she didn't kick something else in the room, after what I said, and by 'something' I mean my head.

Although that might still happen because she's now come charging back into my room.

She squares up to me and her eyes are filled with tears while more pour down her cheeks. "Please do not fuck this up, Michelle." She points a finger at my face and vacates my room yet again.

Well I certainly wasn't expecting such a blatant show of sorrowful emotions from her. Anger, yes. But tears?

Elizabeth and Georgina really are close. And in which case I really had better not fuck this up at all. I've got more than just my own life (lives?) to think about. This is huge. If Doctor Hathor really is planning on killing whoever she wants, then that's outright murder and she must be stopped.

CHAPTER ELEVEN

It's time.

I'm going to sneak into Doctor Hathor's office and find out everything I can about the Girl/Woman and this organisation of hers. Because that's what this place is. She's run this compound as far back as anyone here can remember.

Georgina and Elizabeth are keeping the doctor busy in the tank room. They drained every vat, but none of the women down there are in real jeopardy. We just need Bernice to think that for the time being.

Every woman in the compound is in the tank room. Every woman apart from myself. I'm in deeper than that. I'm below the tank room in the main offices of Doctor Hathor. I've been logged onto the computer and I'm looking through as many files as I can.

After a full minute I'm completely frustrated with myself. I'm not going to find anything this way. There's nothing here. Doctor Hathor's office doesn't hold any secrets. It's a sparsely furnished room with one chair and a desk. And therein lies the question that boggles my mind.

If Bernice really has existed for thousands of years, which I'm not fully accepting into my mind at this moment. But if I stop to think about the implications of such an existence, then I start to realise a whole lot about the woman.

There's no way anyone who's lived for even two lifetimes would have absolutely no decor to their office. Even if this is a place of 'business' there must be something personalised in here somewhere.

Standing, I go to the circular wall. I don't know what I'm looking for on this smooth surface, but I'm sure I'll find something. And if I don't find that something soon, I'm leaving this office with nothing before I risk getting caught.

Ping.

What was that?

I was feeling along the wall and something beeped.

Backtracking, I retrace my footsteps.

Ping.

There it is again, although it's not anything my hands are doing along the wall, it's my foot. I brush the toe of my shoe along the edge. When the ping sounds again I step down, hard.

The floor sinks in under the pressure from my foot and the entire circular wall starts moving round and round. It opens up a space in the wall and I'm facing a new room entirely.

If I thought the room full of tanks was shocking, this room is entirely the opposite, yet in an equally surprising way.

Stepping forward it's as though I'm walking back in time. This entire room is decorated like an ancient Egyptian palace. All the furnishings like tables, chairs, and settees, are all elaborately carved. There are hanging drapes on the walls and items on display that are so authentic they look like ancient artefacts.

Maybe Georgina was right about the rejuvenated age of Doctor Hathor. It makes me wonder if I'm reborn many times my heart will always remain most comfortable with the era in which I was originally first born. Because that's what this room looks like to me; a reflection of the time from which Bernice was first of her mother, and not her own body.

Now this is surely the place I'll find hidden secrets, and after only a little bit of looking around I find her real computer that I sit down at immediately. It's packed with all the information I need. Not only is Bernice planning to kill off women like us, she's been murdering our kind for a very long time already.

This is incredibly disturbing information. I don't understand a lot of what I'm seeing on this computer, but I've discovered files of deceased women and living alike, and that's when I make the mistake of searching my own name.

I'm reading through my data when a soft swishing

noise startles me.

"Interesting reading, Michelle?"

Looking up from the screen I see Doctor Hathor standing on the threshold of her fake office, and she's not alone. There's a muscly looking doctor standing next to her, holding a gun that's aimed at my face.

There's nothing I can do. No where I can go.

Bernice moves slightly to the side. I'm certain she's giving the other woman a clear shot at me. "Your mother really should have told you about your true nature. It was rather unkind of her to up and die on you in that car crash, don't you think?"

"You killed my mother." Standing, I'm filled with anger. "You orchestrated her car accident! You've murdered millions of women!"

The woman to Bernice's left looks about the age of thirty. Her short spiky hair stands on end. She's still pointing the gun at me, but her face contorts questioningly, if only for a second.

I think she's wondering what I'm on about with so much vehemence in my voice.

"Don't shoot me." I look directly at the sturdy doctor. "You don't know what Doctor Hathor has been doing. She's a killer! She's been killing women like us for centuries! Possibly millennia!"

Bernice has the audacity to laugh. "Shoot her."

The woman hesitates and I think I've gotten through to her. When the gun fires though, I realise I was wrong.

I look down at my abdomen in time to see a strange little dart protruding from my flesh, right before I lose consciousness completely.

CHAPTER TWELVE

Waking. Never confused. I won't let my mind slip into unknowing ever again. My brain is intact and I never want to feel like I did that first day upon the lake shore after rejuvenating into a new body.

I sit straight up and immediately take in my surroundings.

Trees everywhere. I'm in the woods. I'm free of the compound and that damned windowless room.

Something isn't right though. My hands are pressed onto a smooth surface. This isn't the ground outside I'm sitting on, it's a smooth black floor.

"What is this?" I scoot backwards and my back hits a wall, but there's nothing there until I look closer.

Glass.

I'm surrounded by glass walls. They are so clear I can see straight through them out into the woods.

How is this happening? How have they trapped me here in this circular room? Because that's what I'm feeling. My hands follow along the glass walls and I've gone round in a wide circle.

"Ouch." My foot hits something.

Turning, I find I've run into myself, or at least the reflection of myself. It's a tiny mirrored protrusion. I find a sunken handle and a door slides open. Inside is a toilet and when I enter the little room I discover its walls are two-way mirrors surrounding a toilet.

This doesn't bode well. How long are they planning to keep me in here?

My answer comes in the form of a noise. I step out of the strange toilet and I can see that part of the circular glass wall is standing open. When I run towards it with plans of escape, I find my way blocked from the outside in the form of the sturdy woman who shot me with a tranquilliser gun. Right before I'm guessing I was inserted into this glass cell.

If I thought I was getting out of here, I thought wrong.

Another girl slides a bag onto the floor of my inner cell and the glass wall closes. From where I'm standing I watch as they both walk away into the woods. They don't travel very far before something strange happens to one of the trees. It splits, half way up its thin trunk of white bark.

This can't be. What I'm seeing is impossible. It's a mirror. A wall of mirrors. The tree didn't split. The girls opened a door in the wall of mirrors. They step through to who-knows-where and vanish when the mirrored door shuts behind them.

Scrabbling for the bag they left behind, I rummage inside and find food and drink.

This is bad. Very, very bad. This can only mean they intend to keep me here for a very long time. I can guess Doctor Hathor won't be allowing me to talk to anyone soon. I'm guessing she can't just kill me, not unless she wants everyone in the compound to know—

That's it! I know where those women disappeared to.

It's the compound itself.

Shoving the uneaten food back into the bag, I close my eyes and lean against the glass wall. I picture the inside of the compound and its own glass walls. From inside the place I must have been looking out into the woods from behind mirrored walls. Glass and see-through on the inside, but mirrors on the outside.

So the compound must be very well hidden. I wonder how far we are from the nearest hamlet, let alone a village or even a town.

If Bernice is thousands of years old, who knows what she's truly capable of after all this time? I can't begin to fathom all she knows with my forty year old brain.

My brain that slithered its way down my back into my new younger body. A transformation that took place as I lay at the bottom of a lake.

These thoughts plague my mind as a constant. I

pace my glass cell day after day, night after starry night, thinking and thinking. Alone with my thoughts and only a gun pointed at my face once per day for company, I'm starting to go insane.

I don't know what day it is when I'm anticipating the arrival of the tranquilizer gun and my delivery of bagged food and water. I've decided that whatever day it is, today will be the day I leave this prison.

When I see the gun-toting woman and another girl dressed as doctors come out of the trees, I ready myself at the place in the glass where I know they'll open part of the wall as a door.

GunWoman makes her stance, aiming the dart-filled weapon where my stomach would be, if I were standing up, which I'm not. I'm crouched and ready to spring.

The wall opens a crack and I push hard. The girl goes flying and before she even lands on her butt I've launched myself into GunWoman.

She grunts and falls with me on top of her. The gun sails through the air and lands upon fallen leaves. I scramble off the woman who screams for help. As I roll I'm able to pick up the gun and run for it.

Dashing round white tree trunks I make my way towards freedom. I don't care if I haven't got a clue where I'm going, I'm just determined to not get captured again. A feat I know is probably impossible considering the fact that I'm chipped. If it comes down to it though, I'll use this gun at point blank range on my head. I'd rather die than be kept in solitary confinement.

Hopefully it won't come to that though. If I can get to a main road somewhere… anywhere… I can wave down a car and get to a hospital. I'll use this weapon if I have to and I'll force a doctor to find whatever tracking chip is implanted in my body.

CHAPTER THIRTEEN

There's a feeling inside me like I know these woods. The further I travel away from my captors, the safer I feel, despite the fact I know they can somehow see my whereabouts with whatever monitoring technology they have on me.

It's night time now. I've stopped running. I'm sat at the base of a tree holding the tranq gun so tight that when I release my fingers they ache. My palm has the imprint of the butt of the gun in my flesh and my skin is bloodless in the moonlight.

Shaking out my fingers I rest until my breathing becomes normal, rather than pumped from so much running.

I never realised how fit I was as a youth. Having a young body again is sure proving useful right about now. I feel as though I could run and run forever. I also feel like I've got a destination. I don't know why I feel compelled to keep going to where it seems I'm being called, but I feel it with my every physical being.

Well that's just crazy. I can't run all over the woods looking for an unknown source of familiarity. I have to get to a main road. If I can at least find a foot trail, it could lead to a dirt road, or a public park somewhere. Yet I have no way of knowing how deep in the woods I am. I know Britain is highly populated, but this country does have wildlands. The unfortunate thing for me is I think I'm lost in woods where there might not be a nearby town around for miles and miles.

My stomach lurches with desperate need. I fight it down and concentrate on finding a road. I listen to the silence of nature at night in hopes I hear the sounds of car wheels upon tarmac.

Nothing, all I hear are owls going toowit-twoo and

shrubs being disrupted by tiny critters.

There's another sound though. Far away in the distance. A liquid sound. A sound of lapping water.

The lake.

It has to be a lake. I know that sound and it combines with this feeling in my gut that I need to go there. Now.

I need to face facts in my mind. I shouldn't have been so impetuous and angry at the compound. I don't know why I feel like the lake is calling me, but I probably could have found that out if I'd bothered to communicate with any of the other women in that mirrored place.

Now I'm just going to have to go it alone, and if I don't get moving soon they'll find me. They could be close to me now, for all I know. I need to get to a hospital. I need to get this tracking chip out of me so I can finally feel free and safe.

Getting to my feet I find renewed strength. It's as though I haven't been running all day over rugged terrain. I'm fighting fit and glad for it. I take off running again and I'm following the sounds of the water. At least if I do go to the nearest lake I can look for a dock. And at the docks are boats, hopefully with people on them who I can ask for help.

CHAPTER FOURTEEN

Someone is following me. I can feel it in my bones. No matter how hard I try to lose them in the night, it's far too bright beneath the full moon to hide anywhere in these woods.

When I feel they're nearly upon me, because I know it's more than one person, I turn to face my pursuers, gun held at arm's length.

"Stop following me or I'll kill you!" I cry out and Georgina steps from the gloom.

"Georgina."

She's not alone.

"Elizabeth."

I still haven't lowered my weapon. They'll know

it's not a real gun if they come any closer. "Don't move."

"Michelle." Georgina ignores my threat. "They're coming for you. You have to let us remove your tracking chip."

That's what I wanted, isn't it? To get this tracking thing out of me so that I can finally be free of these psycho bitches from hell at their compound in the woods. I still don't know if I can trust these two though. For all I know they could be the ones who sold me out. They could have screwed up the draining of the tanks and let me take the fall when I was caught in Bernice's crazy inner sanctum office.

"We don't have time for this!" Elizabeth jumps me.

I try to fight her off but even if my body is young again, I'm not trained in combat or even self-defence, which by now I'm sure Elizabeth is.

She's got me in a good hold and I've lost my grip on the tranquilizer gun entirely. It's fallen into a pile of leaves somewhere and I don't think I'll ever be able to find it again. Certainly not in my current predicament.

"Let me go!" I try to shout but Elizabeth is squashing my lungs.

She presses something hard into my shoulder and suddenly excruciating pain flares beneath my flesh.

"Don't struggle, Michelle." Georgina is close, speaking calmly to me while her cohort tries to murder me with some kind of torture weapon. "It's an electromagnetic syringe. It will pull out the tracking chip that's attached to your collar bone."

"My collar bone? Are you fucking kidding me?" No wonder this hurts so damn bad. I've no choice but to believe what Georgina is telling me is true. And as I grit my teeth against the pain I'm sure as can be that Elizabeth is enjoying every minute of my suffering.

"There." She lifts the black pen-like device from my shoulder. Attached to the tip is an oval shaped glass pill, about the size of an ibuprofen tablet. It's got a red blinking light inside that snuffs out under Georgina's shoe when she stamps on it against a rock.

I'm free. My shoulder hurts like hell and it's

bleeding into my lab coat and shirt, but I don't care. No one will follow me now and I can get the hell out of these woods for good.

"You need to apply pressure to that for five minutes." Georgina instructs me.

"We don't have five minutes." Elizabeth disagrees with her and gets quickly to her feet, finally releasing me from her grasp. "We have to get to the—"

She doesn't get to finish her sentence because Georgina falls into her arms.

Flinging around I watch as Doctor Hathor, the tough blonde woman and more girls come out between trees. They light up their flashlights and aim them straight in our faces. I'm momentarily blinded by the light and blinking I look down at Elizabeth who's fallen to the ground with Georgina in her arms.

Doctor Hathor is on me. She's whispering with venom in my ear. "She's dead. I shot her with a real bullet and if you don't want the same for yourself and Elizabeth I suggest you keep your mouth shut."

She must have used a silencer on her gun because I heard no loud bang. If I believe her at all.

Georgina's eyes are wide open as though staring. Elizabeth didn't hear the doctor just now. No one else did. Only me.

Elizabeth doesn't think Georgina is dead. I don't accept that she's dead. She probably was only shot with a tranq gun.

"Take her." Bernice backs away from me and instructs the girls towards Elizabeth.

In a split second's decision I dive to the ground. I come up winning when my hand finds the tranquilizer gun underneath a pile of leaves. I roll and point it straight at Bernice while still lying on my back, arms outstretched.

I pull the trigger and the gun barely pops any audible sound.

Unfortunately the dart misses its intended target just as the unthinkable happens.

More girls approach, coming out behind trees. They're appropriately dressed for hiking in the woods. I'm still wearing my doctor's garb and so are

Elizabeth and Georgina. I'm not for a second going to believe that Bernice outright killed Georgina in front of all these witnesses. I can't. I just can't wrap my head around that right now. What I can do is act and the only thing I can think of is to roll.

The ravine I plummet down is close enough to get me out of harm's way. Though I'm in a lot of trouble if I break any bones tumbling down this steep hill.

Luckily the fall is short and no one from above has dared follow me down. I wait out capture for hours until the sun starts to rise.

When I come out from beneath tree roots I stumble down a beaten path.

A path! A chance to find civilization!

This path looks familiar and sure enough I'm at Colin's cottage again after an hour's walking.

Colin. I always seem to end up here. How can this be? Is it because I'm close to the lake? The lake sings to me, even now. After everything I've been through I'm forever hearing the lake in my heart. I know why I felt the pull of the lake when my clone was growing inside me. It's because that's our natural way of regenerating. I know this with every fibre of my being and I can't knowingly let Bernice continue the way she is.

I'm only one person but I know if I put my mind to it I can stop her from being in control like this. And I certainly have to do something if she's a murderer.

This is it then. I'm heading towards the cottage and somehow —someway— I'm going to find help.

Colin sees me from inside his kitchen window, the moment I step into his back garden. I don't know why but for some reason seeing him makes me go weak in the knees. I feel exhausted and despite my younger —more physically fit body— I'm still incredibly weakened from all I've endured.

Falling to my knees I collapse onto the grass on my side.

Colin runs out of his cottage. He coughs and comes straight towards me and lifts me into his arms. "What's happened to you?" He carries me inside and lays me on a sofa. I'm fed and watered and I fall asleep shortly thereafter.

I'm in and out of consciousness — dreaming

dreams that I'm no longer suffering. Someone is tending to my wounds.

Half asleep and still very tired, Colin helps me upstairs and into a steaming bath. He cleans me and dresses my shoulder wound, the worst amongst other scrapes and bruises on my brand new body. I've already started accumulating new injuries that will lead to scars. But it doesn't matter, does it? Not in twenty years' time when I rejuvenate again.

And that's what Colin can't do for me. He can't cleans the wounds of my mind. I've had to take so much in these past few days. Wait. Has it been days? I was told the regeneration takes months under water. So how long have I been out here in the woods?

My mind is awhirl. I can no longer relax. I think Colin helps me to bed, but now my dreams cause me to stir every few minutes. When I do manage to sleep it's fitfully and I toss and turn.

Waking in a cold sweat I have to know how long I was asleep. I don't want to keep missing out on days at a time, even if it means I'll get to live many lifetimes in future. That won't count a jot if my brain never screws itself properly into my new body in the first place. Judging by the way I'm not really coping with my own thoughts, I think it's safe to say that I need to prepare myself mentally for each and every day.

I hurry down the stairs that are narrow and thick with cream carpeting. I feel rejuvenated like when I first awoke beside the lake in my new younger body. I don't know what Colin did to me but whatever it was it definitely helped.

"What day is it?" I'm in the kitchen and he's here. "What's the date?"

"It's Friday the twelfth of June."

And then he tells me the year which makes me sit down at the table in despair.

"I have lost a year of my life."

Colin moves toward me. "But you've gained twenty years, if what I was told is true. And I think I'm inclined to believe it now."

I look up at him. "Thank you for helping me."

"Of course."

"You never had to do anything for me. I showed up here when I thought I was pregnant... I seem to break into your home all the time and still you help me. Is there something wrong with you, Colin?" I smile a bit. An act I haven't felt like doing for a very long time. It feels good to do so. It feels good to be able to smile, even just briefly.

"I'm sure there's probably a lot you could find wrong with me, Michelle." Colin returns my smile with one of his own. "But that's probably true of anyone."

"Good point." This is nice. This is casual and normal and nice. I feel like I could sit here and talk to Colin forever, but that can't be, can it? "I need to get back to the compound."

"Georgina and Elizabeth told me about that place." The smile leaves Colin's features, turning into a serious frown that puts a creased line between his eyebrows. "They had their doubts about a Doctor Hathor?"

They really did tell him a lot. "Why were you so conversational with them? Why are you letting me sit in your kitchen now?"

He gets to his feet and starts making tea, facing away from me. "Because I've always sort of known. I've lived by this lake for quite some time now, Michelle. I've seen girls... women like you before."

I jump to my feet in astonishment. "You've seen women rejuvenate? So when I showed up here pregnant, you knew?"

Colin turns round to face me. "I didn't know for certain, but I had my theories. One of which was that I was going crazy. I'm a writer. Since moving out here I thought it was my overly vivid imagination playing tricks on me, and then there was you..."

"And then Elizabeth shot at you."

"Yes, there was that too."

"I guess you sort of fell into getting very involved, and it's all my fault."

The smile returns to his lips at my comment and I'm wondering what he thinks is funny at this particular junction in time.

Colin hands me a hot cup of tea. "I'm okay with that if it means it's your fault we met."

I take a sip and the liquid warms me inside. Luckily it's still early morning or I'd never be able to drink this by lunchtime when the sun is hot and high in the sky. It's been an unusually hot summer this year and…

Suddenly I don't have the strength to stand on my own two feet. I collapse into the chair, nearly spilling my tea before I set it down properly on the table.

"Are you okay?" Colin abandons his drink on the counter and comes toward me.

He's on one knee and it's a good thing too. I feel so weak I can't even hold up my head. I slide into Colin's arms and nearly fall asleep. He picks me up and carries me into the sitting room. I'm lain onto the sofa and he sits next to me, my head rests on his shoulder.

"I don't know what's wrong with me." My eyes are closed, my voice is strained. "Whenever I think about the date my head gets all muddled up."

It's not a hot summer this year, is it? Because it's not the same summer at all. I keep forgetting I've missed a year.

"Those women said something about your brain reconnecting. They said your thoughts will affect you physically after your first rejuvenation."

"They said that?" What else did Georgina and Elizabeth tell Colin? I wonder. "So my head won't be screwed on right for the next twenty years?"

This is making me panic and my brain feels fuzzier than ever.

"I don't think so. Maybe you should rest now, Michelle. They said it's only for the first couple of years."

Yes. Rest. I definitely need to do that again soon. But how much sleep am I going to need? And if my brain is going to continue to be wacky for another year, how will I cope? If it weren't for Colin's help right now, I'd have no one. Mum is dead and I never knew my father. I lost all my friends a few months before my stomach started showing the false pregnancy. I wasn't wanted by anyone.

"I hope they told you something else."

"Ssshhh." Colin urges me to sleep.

"Just one more question, please."

Sighing loudly, he eventually agrees to answer me.

"Did Georgina and Elizabeth mention anything about being unwanted before the clone starts to grow?"

"You mean at age forty, or so?"

I can barely manage to shake my head yes now against his chest.

"They said that's your body's way of keeping its own evolutionary secret from Homo sapiens who are unable to rejuvenate."

So I was unwanted as an act of self-preservation and not because of what I thought. I was almost at my wits end when I thought everyone hated me, but it was how my body works; physically ostracizing people so that they'd leave my life before the change. Before I could return to them as my younger self, thereby raising a lot of questions.

And I do have seemingly endless questions about the new me, but I'm not going to get to ask any more right now. I'm just too tired and I can't help but fall into a deep sleep.

CHAPTER FIFTEEN

I'm groggy for days and days. I make sure Colin informs me of the date so I don't lose track of time. It helps to keep me sane and my energy increases as the days pass. I feel like I'm being selfish by not going straight back to the compound. But I can't go anywhere, or do anything for anyone, in this state. For now I have to rest. I'll be able to make plans to return to the compound later. It's no good worrying about Georgina, or Elizabeth, even if that woman/girl is a total bitch; I can now somewhat understand her crazy attitude.

Somewhat.

"Thank you for this." It's morning time and I'm

lying on my side in bed with the pillow scrunched up under my head. "Thank you for everything, Colin."

He smiles and leans forward on his chair that he's scooted up next to the bed. He coughs a couple times into his palm that he brings up to cover his mouth. "It's okay, I don't mind sleeping on the sofa in my own house for nearly a week. Think nothing of it, Michelle."

I know he's joking. I'm the one who insisted I should be sleeping on the couch, but he wasn't having it so I have his bed. "No point in trying to guilt trip me now, mister. It was your bad decision to take the sofa." I roll around pretending to be super comfy.

"Now you're just being mean." He laughs.

"I think this bed is the most comfortable thing I've ever slept on!" I'm actually not lying, but I think I've gone too far now. Colin stands and makes a grand show of rubbing his sore back.

He's funny this guy. He's also very good looking. He's so charismatic and I find myself getting more and more curious about him every day I'm confined to this bed. "So why do you live all the way out here in the woods?"

Eyebrows are raised now. Colin doesn't answer me straight away. He busies himself by adjusting the duvet for a few minutes first. "I'm a writer, I enjoy the solitude immensely."

"I used to have writer friends. They lived in the city just fine."

He shrugs. "Well, that's great for them."

I think I've said something wrong. He's not very open when it comes to me asking questions about his personal life. Then again, who is? I should probably stop being so nosy. I've had nothing but help from this guy and I don't want to offend him if he thinks I'm prying.

"Yeah, that is good for them. And let them to it. They weren't exactly there for me anyway, not when I was nearing forty. I don't know what my body did. Maybe it gives out really bad body odour when the clone starts to grow, or something like that."

At this Colin bursts out laughing. It's a nice sound, his laugh, and it makes me smile endlessly.

When he's done chuckling he sits next to me on the edge of the bed. "Thank you, Michelle."

He's thanking me? "For what? You're the one who's been doing everything for me."

"Thank you for coming into my life. I was ready to end it right when you showed up."

He what?

If I had the energy I'd sit straight up right now.

"I'm sorry." He stands again and walks toward the window. "I shouldn't have sprung that on you. Especially not now while you're so weak in the mind."

"Are you calling me weak-minded?"

When he turns back to me I'm ready with a smile.

It's worked. I think he knows he can confide in me.

"I'll have you know I was a highly successful composer before my body decided to grow another one inside itself. Okay so maybe my job was to synthesize filler music for film sequences, but that does take a lot of creativity, you know. And I was the best at what I did."

Well that was a hell of a speech. Colin just revealed to me that he was contemplating suicide and all I can do is ramble on about my former job?

"I'm sure you were."

He's coming back. He's sitting on the bed again.

"Why did you want to die?"

There. I've blurted out the question of questions. I don't think he's going to pull away and if he does he'll have to escape my hand that I've placed atop his.

Looking down, he intertwines his fingers through mine.

I wasn't expecting that. I like it. I like his nearness a lot.

When Colin next speaks he can't meet my eyes. "I have terminal cancer."

My eyes close instantly over wet tears.

Life is so unfair.

Here I am just discovering that I could possibly live forever. I meet this amazing man only to find out his lifespan is going to be cut shorter than normal.

I'm suddenly angry and my eyelids fly open. "I didn't want to know that. I take back my question. Damn you…"

My voice chokes on a sob and now I'm crying over a guy I just met. I sit up and tears pour down over my cheeks. I stand up in the bed and look down at Colin. I'm breathing heavily in and out, trying to stop myself from crying like a baby.

I can't though. I'm overwhelmed. I can't stop thinking, wondering how long he has to live. Wondering why I had to turn out to be some kind of cloned freak. Everything is piling into my brain as sorrow. It's pumping emotions and hormones through my veins. I can feel my synapses firing and when I close my eyes again I see bolts of lightning cross my vision.

"Michelle."

Open my eyes. Look down at Colin.

"You… you're glowing."

What is he saying? I can hear his words but my brain isn't able to translate them into anything coherent. And what is that light? It's filling me up. I feel warm. Like there's something inside me bursting to be freed.

No more thoughts, just do.

Colin is staring at me as I kneel before him. I notice my hand as it goes to his chest. There's something strange about my hand, but I don't understand what it is I'm seeing. It's my own flesh, but somehow it's different.

I open Colin's shirt and he doesn't move away from me. I put my other hand on the skin of his chest, along with the other. All the feeling of warmth in my body pushes through my veins and up into my palms. Then I feel it slide through to Colin's flesh, making him take in a deep breath of air.

His eyes close when my hands cool down. He falls to the side and lies down on the bed. He's asleep as soon as his head hits the pillow and now I'm the one who's wide awake looking down upon a man I've come to care deeply for.

CHAPTER SIXTEEN

It's night. The room is darkened and the only light that shines is coming through the window from the stars above.

Colin woke about an hour ago and I've been lying next to him in his bed.

Blink. Blink. Blink.

His eyes start moving rapidly and all of a sudden he inhales deeply. When he lets out all that air, he speaks. "You healed me."

"What are you talking about?"

"You were glowing and… and then these sparkly things moved from your hands into me… and now I can breathe!"

"I think you'll find you've been breathing this whole time. At least while I've known you."

The smile is back on his face, I can see it even in the dark.

"You're a silly woman right now who looks like a young girl. I never would have even believed you could clone yourself, let alone that you had magical healing powers—"

"Whoa now. Hold on there a minute, mister—"

Colin sits up and turns to me with exuberance. He gently grabs both of my hands and kisses each of my palms.

I'm taken aback, but not unpleasantly so. "I saw what you did to me, Michelle. I saw it and I feel it now. Look… I mean listen…"

And I do listen as he breathes fully in and out.

Come to think of it, his chest does sound clear. I did slightly wonder why he coughs all the time.

"Wait. Do you have lung cancer?"

"I did have lung cancer until you healed me from it."

Not this again. I do wish I knew what he was on

about. "Are you being serious about my body glowing? I did feel really strange—"

"I'm one hundred percent serious."

I look into his eyes. Light from outside the window makes them sparkle with happiness. He's still grasping my hands and I feel invigorated.

"I'm not sleepy anymore." I whisper and look down at his mouth.

He's leaning towards me and now he's finally let go of my hands, but it's only so he can cup the back of my neck. He presses his lips to mine and the warmth of his kiss makes me realise I really am fully awake and aware.

The sensation is broken, but only momentarily while Colin runs into the bathroom and quickly brushes his teeth. When he comes out I'm kneeling on the bed waiting for him.

He kisses me again. His tongue pushes in past my open lips and I taste mint on his breath. I can feel him relishing every bit of air he takes in and out through his lungs. It's as though he's breathing me in, pulling me further into his kiss with the fact that his chest feels strong and clear.

This time when I pull away it's to slowly remove his clothes. As I do so I touch my skin to his and by the time I'm finished my palms feel as heated as they did when I touched him with all my being.

Colin takes my wrists gently in his hands. He kisses my palms again. He doesn't make any comments about light pouring off me, so I'm guessing that whole glowing skin conversation is on hold for the time being, which is perfectly fine by me. I can't get enough of his touch right now and I want more of him immediately.

He releases my wrists and I slip out of his dressing gown I've been wearing. He touches my young skin everywhere and my hormones rage up like teenager all over again.

Colin's touch soon comes from his lips. He licks and kisses me down past my neck. His tongue laps at my breasts and when he breathes out heavily my nipples harden in response.

His kisses travel down over my tummy. When his mouth descends further I too suck in a deep breath of air.

I'm in ecstasy as Colin's tongue licks and sucks at my most sensitive place. He traces my inner and outer folds gently, wetting me before pushing two fingers inside.

Over and over, in and out, his fingers twist slightly while his tongue works its magic on the most sensualized part of my body. I want this pleasure to go on forever but I know I'll burst with orgasm too soon if I let him continue.

Pushing up I move onto my knees as comes up too. I put my hand around his seven inch long erection. It's hot and pulsing in my palm. I kiss him on the mouth and the scent and taste of me lingers there. Stroking his hardness for a moment makes him moan with pleasure and I let go slowly. I turn around and get onto all fours.

He's certainly not a man who needs telling. His hands caress my bare bottom before he feels the moisture between my legs. Pushing close I feel him press the tip of his swollen member at the opening where I'm wettest. He thrusts into me, gently at first, and then he quickens the pace.

Our breathing matches each other's gasp for release. He slows pace again, sliding out, then thrusting up hard inside me. It punches the air from my lungs and I cry out wanting more.

"Michelle." He says my name on a whisper. His need becomes a rapid pace again in wanting for climax.

Hormones race through my veins. I'm hot and tingly with each thrust of his smooth, hardness. It's all moving in and through me.

When the height of pleasure explodes within me, it blasts out through every fibre of my being. And this time I see it. My body is alight with a gentle bluish glow. I can see in the reflection of the wall mirror as Colin continues to push in and out. The glow from my body enters through him sending pulses of light throughout. We both shudder and cry out with a final release of shared orgasm like nothing I've ever experienced before.

CHAPTER SEVENTEEN

Lazily I trace my finger over Colin's chest as I rest my head on his shoulder, in bed. It's early morning now and I'm feeling more rejuvenated than ever. I feel as though my mind has finally come into myself and if it took an act of love-making to ensure that happened, then I'm all for it.

Colin and I shared something almost magical, even though I know that's not true. I want to pretend it's so for just a while before I have to start wondering at what my new body is truly capable of.

"You allowed me to experience a woman's orgasm, Michelle." Colin has been flabbergasted about this all night and into the morning. His love-making didn't stop until we'd sated each other many more times throughout the night. "It was combined with my own climax and I've never known such pleasure existed!"

I felt him too. It was as though our orgasms mingled and poured into each other through fucking.

So much physicality. My body and brain are as one again. I'm fully renewed and connected with life on a higher level of some kind. There are still unanswered questions I hold in my heart, but I know I can find answers without having to ask anyone at the compound. Their methods are clinical and out of tune with the natural way of our bodies. I know this now. I rejuvenated in the lake like was meant to be. I'm forever called to the lake, it's now a part of who I am.

Yet I do have to return to the compound. The ways of Doctor Hathor cannot be allowed to continue. I will expose her to all the women there. Surely they won't stay if they know the truth about their murderous leader.

"I feel amazing." I speak to Colin with a clear

head. "I'm ready to go back."

"Go back where?"

"To the compound, of course. I told you what's happening there."

No immediate response from my new lover is forthcoming. But finally, he replies. "Well I'm going with you."

"You can't, there are no men there. They have the grounds monitored, I'm sure. Hell, they're probably monitoring the whole world with their technology. They'll see you coming a mile off and then I'll never get in."

"And how are you planning to slip past their defences?"

"Easy." I sit up in bed and grab a pillow. I'm stark naked so I don't have a shirt to stuff it under. I press it to my belly and pretend I'm pregnant. "They'll think I'm expecting to clone and I'll be wearing a hoodie so they won't see my face."

"You've thought this all through, I see." Colin doesn't seem convinced. He sits up too and quickly licks my nipple.

"Stop, you silly." I don't really want him to stop, but if he doesn't I'll never get out of this bedroom, let alone back into the woods to find the compound. I'm determined to retrace my steps though, and I have a feeling after wandering around looking pregnant they're bound to find me eventually.

CHAPTER EIGHTEEN

I'm out in the woods, again. Alone.

I've been travelling with my head down for hours in the general direction from which I came from the compound. At least I think I am. Not only is my body in tune with going towards the lake, but it's as though I can feel when I pull myself away from it. And I also somehow feel connected to other women like me. It doesn't feel like I'm randomly wandering towards getting myself forever lost in these woods. I sense that I know where I'm going.

And I also sense that I'm not as alone as I thought. I have a feeling Colin is following me.

Dammit. He's going to ruin everything. They'll

spot him for sure. I'm certain these woods are crawling with hidden cameras. I've fallen in love with the guy down to the deepest levels of my being, but I'm also connected to the women at the compound on an evolutionary level too. I can't just let Bernice continue the way she has. Who knows what other evil secrets and misdeeds she's held over the centuries? I can't knowingly carry on with my life if she's left to her own devices. I have to speak out. I have to help in any way I can.

Keeping my head down under the hoodie I borrowed from Colin, I hold my stomach where there's a pillow stuffed under my shirt. I'm wearing the shoes from the compound but I borrowed a pair of Colin's jeans that are too long for me, so hopefully the shoes won't be noticed.

There's more rustling noises and I'm sure it's Colin who's about to give me away entirely.

"Are you all right?"

A girl's voice. It isn't Colin.

"No." I whimper in reply, pretending to be lost. "The lake called to me. Where am I?"

"Don't worry. I know what you're going through." The girl's voice is soothing, she means to try and comfort me so she must be from the compound. "I'm sure you have many questions and I can answer them for you if you'll come with me."

I nod my head and pull the hoodie further down over my face. "Don't look at me!" I'm putting up the pretence that I'm confused and I don't want her to see my face.

The girl takes my arm and guides me away. We walk together for less than a mile and suddenly I hear a swishing sound.

It's the mirrored door to the entrance of the compound. It's standing open and I'm being taken inside.

"Just wait here while I get a nurse."

The girl leaves me in a hospital-like room, similar to the one I stayed in after rejuvenating. She never saw my face before she left the room and I didn't see what she looked like either.

Springing into action I leap off the bed and throw off my hood. I pull out the pillow and leave it on the floor. I'm out the door and hurrying down the circular corridor before I realise I'm quite conspicuous dressed like this. I find an empty hospital room with a stash of scrubs in the cupboard. I change quickly and then I'm en route once again to the tanks below ground. I don't know what I'm going to do once I get there, but I'll figure that out later.

When a young doctor has her face scanned by the lift, I take my chance and step through the doors with her.

I'm waiting for her to sound an alarm but the girl doesn't take her eyes off the tablet in her hand. She's busy poking and sliding her finger across the screen and it's got me curious as to what's so interesting on that iPad.

Leaning slightly to the right I peer over her shoulder.

She's flicking through photos and I almost cry out when I see the images.

There are pictures of my mother on that screen. What is she doing with photos of my mother? When she flicks to the next image it's a picture of me with my mum.

I'm standing slightly behind this girl and something changes in her facial features. She frowns in concentration and starts turning her head round.

Before she can see my face I react when the elevator door opens.

I grab the tablet. "I need to borrow that, mine's playing up."

Making sure my head is down and my hair fallen in front of my face, I dash out of the lift, iPad in my hands.

"Hey!" The girl shouts from behind me. "You'd better take that back to reception point one when you're finished, or they'll have my ass."

An American girl.

I leave her quickly behind heading straight into the rows of water-filled tanks. I fully intend on trying to get into Bernice's office again. If I can download the information I need off the computer from her inner sanctum, I can spread it through email on this tablet.

Then everyone will know what she's up to.

I have no idea when Doctor Hathor will be going

into or coming out of her lower-level office, so I'm going to have to wait her out by the door to her lift.

CHAPTER NINETEEN

I've been waiting for hours sitting at the base of a tank. A deformed shape floats inside the glass vat as a remnant of something that used to be, and will again be a human (looking) female.

The hum of gentle power rumbles through my chest. Occasional bubbling noises makes me feel like I'm in an aquarium if I close my eyes. I'm passing the time by perusing the images on this tablet. I don't know what they're doing here until I read the accompanying documents. There are warning messages about reporting any sightings of my mother, should she be found.

Scrolling to the date I notice this memo just went

out this morning, but my mother is dead, so it doesn't make much sense.

Someone's coming. I hear voices and they're not just inside my age forty head.

I scoot down a few tanks and listen.

"We'll have to warn everyone, but I think it's Michelle."

That's Bernice and she's talking about me.

"I'm sorry, Doctor Hathor." A girl replies. "I thought she was a wanderer. I didn't want her going off and finding the lake."

"Don't worry, Darla. This is a good thing. We've been looking for Miss Locke. We wanted her here, just probably not like this."

Bernice laughs and it's a fake sound. I think she's quite annoyed that this girl Darla managed to bring me into the compound and then let me fully escape the hospital-like room.

They're both very close to me now. I've been waiting by the entrance to Doctor Hathor's underground office. I'm already deep underground, but her secret sanctum is housed even lower. I have no way of knowing how Bernice got this place built. I can only contemplate as to how much power she wields across the world after existing for such a long time.

Thinking such thoughts does my head in about the future. I must remember not to dwell on the weirdness of my newly discovered nature, lest it drive me crazy from my recently merged brain into new cranium metamorphosis.

"Why's she so damned important anyway?"

I think Darla detects falsity in Doctor Hathor's demeanour as well. The inflection in her young voice suddenly sounds untrusting.

"You know why, Darla. Michelle Locke risks exposing us to the world, and then what would we do? Tell me, do you want to be experimented on?"

There's a momentary silence, broken soon enough by Darla's reply. "Obviously I don't, but one woman isn't going to expose us all."

"You'd be surprised what one woman is capable of."

I'm pretty sure Doctor Hathor is referring to

herself now.

There's a bleeping sound and I listen as the door to Bernice's personal lift slides open. The two women step inside and I'm about to take action when I'm grabbed from behind. My captor has a hand over my mouth until I hear the elevator door close.

"Ssshhh, Michelle, don't scream."

That voice. It's as familiar to me as my own. When my mouth is released I whirl around.

Tears spring into my eyes. "Mum?" I look at her, grabbing her by the shoulders quite hard. I fear if I don't secure her physically, she'll float away and disappear as the ghost she has to be. "You're alive?"

She nods and we embrace. I won't let her go. Tears of confused joy pour down my face. "But you died in a car crash. You left me, Mum." I'm sobbing now. Quietly. Bewildered.

"This is all Berenice's doing." Mum says Doctor Hathor's first name a bit funny, but I barely notice. "She has been afraid of me for a very long time, Michelle."

Mum pulls back and wipes the tears off my cheeks

with her hand. "And she fears you too now as well."

Fears?

Between sniffles I try to speak. "Why would she fear us?"

"Because we're more than she could ever be."

Mum's not making much sense right now, but I don't really care. I'm just amazed she's alive. I don't think the shock of her presence has hit me fully, and I'll be glad if it never does. I missed my mum so much and now I never have to miss her again, unless...

"I was told we die if we get pregnant for real."

Mum angles her head at my statement, questioningly.

"You gave birth to me instead of a clone forty years ago," I continue. "So having me as a real baby means—"

"I won't die of old age, Michelle."

Now I'm more confused than ever. I sink down to the floor again and mum sits next to me. She strokes my hair comfortingly for a while, until I look up at her lined and wrinkled face. Her dark hair is shot through with streaks of grey. I don't need her to placate my feelings right now. She's telling me she won't die, but I know the opposite to be true, from what I've been told.

"You don't believe me, do you?" Mum looks at me and it's like she can read my thoughts. She's always been able to do that. She knows me so well. "Here, let me show you."

Mum lifts her hand as though she doesn't want me to leave her hanging for a high five.

Frowning, I put my hand up too. She puts her hand onto mine and something incredible happens.

Glowing blue specs light up between our skins the way phytoplankton makes a tropical beach glow at night.

"Is this magic?"

"No, Michelle. It's biology."

I watch as my mother's face transforms right before my eyes. Her wrinkles vanish and the grey in her hair fades to dark brown. It's long to her shoulders over her white lab coat.

Mum takes a deep breath and takes her hand away.

When she does the little lights go out and she's young again. My age.

"Your beautiful face, Mum. What did you do?" I loved every line in my mother's features, but of course I should have known she was ab-normal, like me. Or rather, I'm not a normal human female like her.

"I've been able to regenerate with my offspring like this for centuries, hon. And you will be able to as well. That's why Berenice kept me here. She's been experimenting on me ever since she captured me and falsified my disappearance with a car accident cover story. Berenice wants what you and I naturally possess within our biology, Michelle. She wants to take it, but she hasn't been able to unlock our genetic secrets. She doesn't know that I'm the one who can give her this gift, because she was never a good enough person to just ask."

That was quite a spiel. So much to remember and I can't take it all in while staring at my mother's new young face.

"You can do this too, Michelle. And you can bond

with a partner physically when you meet someone you love."

"I already have." I tell her about Colin, leaving out the more explicit details of our joining. This is still my mother, even if she looks like she could be my sister now.

"Isn't this touching?"

Bernice.

She's come round one of the tanks with the girl who brought me in from the woods.

We both rise to our feet. I step in front of my mother, defensively. This witch won't take my mum from me again. The girl next to her looks freaked out. Her long red hair is pulled back in a tight ponytail and I'm wondering just how much this young lady likes to emulate Bernice.

"I don't know why you're filling your own daughter's head with such lies, Nastasen."

What did she call my mother? Her name has always been Natasha, but that's only the name I've known her by throughout my life, which is short in comparison to what I now know.

"Ladies." Doctor Hathor says one word and many girls appear from behind tanks. "Take them."

"No, don't do this Berenice, not again!" My mother cries out as I'm swiftly removed from her presence.

I'm jabbed with something sharp as a needle in my neck and everything goes dark.

CHAPTER TWENTY

Waking. Outdoors. Lost.

I'm in the woods. There are trees all around. I'm lying flat on my back staring up at the leafy canopy above. It must be evening time, judging by the light of the fading sun in the sky.

A mosquito flies close to my ear, creating an irritating buzzing noise. I slap the insect away as it lands on my cheek. This causes me to sit straight up and my head spins in the process. Birds chirp pleasantly all around, juxtaposing my inner confusion.

There's a scent on the air, one of smoke and hot metal in the distance. Burning things. Things are burning far away.

I don't know my own identity for a while. I can't even contemplate my whereabouts until the pain in my head stops throbbing at least a little bit. I do the only thing I can think of right now, and that is to wait.

Just breathe.

Relax.

Now think this through.

I remember my mother. My mother is alive! She was taken from me again. Or I was taken from her? I don't know. What am I doing out here? How did I get here? I was last in the compound deep underground.

"Michelle."

"Colin? How did I get here?"

The man, my new lover has scrambled close to me on the ground.

"I brought you here. I went back to check on the woman who said she was your mother."

"My mum! Is she okay?" I grab his shirt in desperation and it's now I notice he reeks of smoke and there's a shadow of soot on the side of his face. "What's going on?"

"I don't know where she is." Colin collapses and sits down beside me, hard. I release his shirt. "I didn't know what happened. I followed you but you disappeared with that girl into the trees. Then the trees started smoking and women began to appear out of nowhere!"

He must have followed me into the woods when I specifically told him not to, but if he hadn't followed me, would I be here now?

"What smoke?" He must be talking about the compound with its outer walls made of mirrors. "Is the compound on fire?"

"The compound?"

"The place where they let women transform. My mother!"

Quickly I get to my feet and I'm off and running straight away.

"Hang on, Michelle." Colin follows me. "You're mum told me to keep you safe!"

And who's going to keep my mother safe? She

wasn't safe from Bernice before and if the compound is on fire she certainly won't be safe all the way down there in the buried confines.

We reach the smoking reflections in the woods. Women and girls are sprawled on the ground everywhere, coughing, retching, and helping each other if they can.

"Elizabeth!" I cry out and head straight for the blonde girl. She's tending to a girl on the ground.

"Mum!" I kneel down just as my mother sits up.

"I'm okay, Michelle."

"What happened?" Colin approaches, running his hands through his hair.

"I'll tell you what happened." Elizabeth stands. "My mother is dead!"

I roll backwards just as her foot flies toward the spot where my head used to be.

"What are you playing at you fucking bitch?" My eyes are wide with confused anger. I'm crouched down, right before I spring up onto my feet with the agility and ease of being youthful again.

I'm not fast enough, and neither is Colin. He

lunges forward but not in time for Elizabeth to catch me across the jaw in a massive punch.

My head bows to the side and by the time I straighten again both my mother and Colin have Elizabeth locked down.

"Elizabeth please." My mother placates the bitch. "We have to stick together now."

"Let me go." Elizabeth isn't struggling to be freed any more. I can hear her words but I refuse to look her in the eye. "I'm doing this to help you, Natasha, and no one else."

Why is she so willing to help my mother? I wonder.

"What is going on?" Finally, I lift me head. I look at Colin who I'm sure wants answers too.

"Elizabeth set off the failsafe destruct mechanism." My mother has let Elizabeth go and so has Colin. I'm keeping my distance from the blonde girl. "It flushes the compound with fire, and then water pipes in from the lake. It floods each rejuvenation chamber and fills the entire complex, putting out the flames."

"Is that where the water comes from and gets drained to?" I'm thinking about each tank that holds a transforming woman inside it. "So the lake water comes into each vat?"

My mother nods her head and Elizabeth leaves. She goes off and to my surprise she starts helping girls in distress. She's a strange one, that young looking woman. One minute she's trying to kill me and the next she's helping everyone else within her sights.

"Georgina's dead?" Suddenly the realisation of her words hits me.

"Berenice killed her." Mum answers my question. "And she won't hesitate to kill many more if it means keeping our secret and discovering mine."

The secret of our rejuvenation. All of us. And the secret of what my mother and I can do besides being able to live young again.

I explain it to Colin. He seems to believe every word I've said. He did experience the strange gift I gave him between us, so he doesn't need convincing.

"Where is Bernice now?"

Mum looks at me with concern watering up her eyes. I know she's a strong woman, my mother is, but even if she has existed for what seems like an eternity, she's still just a girl who feels profoundly. Perhaps she's capable of feeling more than I'll ever know. With time, I wonder what my countenance will be like as far as handling situations goes.

How do any of these women cope with living for so long and all that entails?

"I don't know." My mum finally answers Colin.

I look around at the girls, the women girls. "Why is she out to kill me?"

Mum looks where I'm gazing and spots Elizabeth. "She's not. She's just confused. Most of them are. Berenice has been controlling these women for a very long time."

"Controlling?"

"Yes. It's not the natural way for us to rejuvenate in glass chambers inside a laboratory. We all need the lake. There are things in the lake that contribute to our transformation. Berenice never understood that, even in the beginning."

SUZ KORB

We get everyone back inside the ground floor of the burnt out and previously flooded compound. It's a sight like a spectacle that I don't want to contemplate cleaning up. It's fine though, I'm sure after mum has a word with everyone here, no one will ever come back.

"What about the women below levels?" I ask my mother while helping a girl sit against the wall.

"They're tethered to each glass chamber. Even when the compound flooded they were okay and their tanks have refilled with lake water just fine."

"Everyone!" Elizabeth is at the nurse's terminal. She's standing high up on a chair clapping her hands loudly. "Your re-lives are about to change, but it's for the better. You have to listen to Natasha now."

I look at Mum. She purses her lips and then sighs loudly. "It's time for you all to know the truth." She puts a hand on my shoulder and then takes the floor where Elizabeth was standing.

Drips plop down from the walls and ceilings. The stench of stale smoke is heavy in the damp air. Puddles have formed here and there along the length

144

of the corridor but no one much cares about their own comfort right now. No one is critically injured and we're all rapt with attention on my mother because at this very moment her whole body is lit up in a gentle blue glow.

CHAPTER TWENTY-ONE

THE PAST

More than two-thousand years ago Queen Berenice was forced to leave her kingdom of Egypt. The people loved her, but they would not if they knew of the illegitimate babe growing within her womb. This child that was suddenly there inside her, despite her never having lain with a man.

She put up the ruse of marrying again. Berenice chose a King who was responsible for the genocide and slaughter of many. She then let it be known that after her wedding her new husband killed her. While she herself escaped Egypt alone. The people revolted against her murderer, the new King. They killed him within a matter of days.

But Berenice was not to know this. She had already left the continent due to the shame she felt because of the size of her womb.

Where she went was North West. She didn't know how she knew where she was going, but she knew where she would end up.

Once she reached her destination many months later her womb was large enough to nearly burst her belly wide open.

She sat near a lake in her new environment. The air was damp and cool. The trees all around the lake shore were darkest green. Her body was flaming with heat from inside and she knew the only way to cool down was to get into the water of the lake.

As she took off the skins and furs that were her clothing, she heard a strange noise. Looking up she saw a woman crawling naked —and heavily pregnant— towards the same shore.

When the woman was there with her, they both crawled into the water together. One last nod of their heads to each other before they both dived down.

And down and down and down.

Berenice's body cooled. Her giant belly felt weightless. She closed her eyes, took in a deep breath of lake water and felt ready to die.

But she did not die. She lived and she slept.

The body inside her was not that of a baby. It was the small form of herself repeated. As her new body grew, her old body began to transform.

Her old skull opened up at the back of her head, with only a thin layer of skin remaining.

When the newly gestated and fully formed body in Berenice's womb reached maximum height and prime age, her brain began its decent.

It moved out of the skull of her old body, protruding in a deformed lump at the base of her neck. Over time the brain slowly moved down the spine, still as a protrusion. All the while her old body disintegrated, providing the new body with nutrients.

When the brain reached the open skull of the new body, it was no longer the womb of a woman the new body was encased in. It was now a sphere of flesh.

The brain inserted itself into the new body and over more time it connected with the spinal cord and became the body itself.

CHAPTER TWENTY-TWO

When Berenice woke she was not dead under the water. She was resting face down on the pebbled shore of the lake.

And someone else rested beside her.

It was the woman who went into the water with her. She was asleep on her front and she was no longer large with child.

Berenice knew that she could not be lain upon her stomach if it too was quick with babe. She rolled onto her back and felt her stomach. It was flat and no life grew within her. The skin of her shrunken womb felt more taught than it had been in a long time. Berenice looked over at the woman again. She saw the stark difference that she didn't notice before.

The woman was no longer a woman, but now a girl.

Her dark brown hair wet and plastered to her face. Her skin young and supple. But it was her. Berenice knew it was the same woman who was pregnant from before they went into the water.

She woke her then. She learned of her name.

Nastasen. From her own world of Egypt. Nastasen had also travelled far and wide to be here.

The two women formed a bond over the years that was unbroken by man or beast. No one came between their friendship and when their bodies were once again older and swollen of belly, the two women left the tribe and went again to the woods.

They sunk their heated bodies below the water. Every time they were renewed again as youths in body, but not in mind, their rejuvenation periods grew shorter and shorter.

Berenice grew tired of the lake. She had taught herself how to regain power and she longed for the status of Queen that her original self was born into.

The Roman invasion of her new land enabled her chances at prestige. And now the friendship with Nastasen saw its first tears of their bonded cord of trust.

Nastasen continued to rejuvenate in the lake every twenty —or so— years. Berenice went her own way and became a woman of great power and status. She had the lake water brought to her.

More women came to the woods over time. Berenice wanted to control them all. She built up ways to contain the women as their bodies transformed, far away from the lake.

Nastasen always returned to the lake and over a thousand years her new body transformed naturally. The lake not only renewed her youth, but it gave her abilities to heal and heal others. To communicate with out words to the men she loved. New abilities with every rejuvenation.

Berenice discovered Nastasen's enhancements after hundreds of years had passed. She attempted to harness what she thought were powers due to her as a woman of great standing in the world, whatever era.

Nastasen was Natasha now and Berenice became Bernice. Both women, all women who could rejuvenate learned how to blend into society. They were constantly going away from friends and lovers to contain the secret of their longevity.

Except for Natasha. She grew the ability to have offspring without aging and dying herself.

Bernice knew nothing but rage when she first began to experiment on Natasha.

In the nineteenth century Natasha was Bernice's captive. But no matter the advanced machinery, Bernice could not extrapolate Natasha's secret abilities to claim them as her own.

CHAPTER TWENTY-THREE
PRESENT DAY

I'm shocked to my core at the tale my mother has just told us all. I cannot begin to fathom her existence as a woman who has rejuvenated for thousands of years.

"Berenice…" My mother stops and clears her throat. "I'm sorry, you all know her as Bernice. She is responsible for much death, but her reign has now come to an end."

Her reign? Yes, my mother is definitely very old in the brain, despite looking young in her rejuvenated flesh.

An almighty crash erupts around us. The

incredible sound blasts through the core of my being. I duck down and cover my head with my arms as every mirrored glass wall explodes and cracks, showering glass down onto the ground in massive pile of rubble that sparkles in the sunlight.

Some girls scream. Chaos all around.

"Nastasen!"

It's Bernice. She's standing on the outside of the collapsed wall of mirrors. The way she keeps screeching my mother's original name sounds like a woman filled with rage and loathing.

She's not alone.

The ginger-haired girl is there, along with muscly looking women surrounding the entire compound. They collectively step over the glass rubble and crunch their way forward, all dressed as though they're ready for battle in army fatigues and heavy boots.

Bernice grabs my mother and the soft glow of her blue form goes out. "I know you can give your powers to me. Now push them out or I will end you and you'll never rejuvenate again."

I leap to my feet, but just as I'm about to attack Bernice I'm grabbed from behind by Red.

"Do what she says or your daughter dies."

There's a gun pointed at my head. Not even Colin dares come closer from behind when I spot him in my peripheral.

"Do you want to be responsible for more deaths, Nastasen?" Berenice shoves her teeth against my mother's ear. She hisses low, but I can still hear her enraged voice. "It was always your fault, Nastasen. Every woman I killed is on your head. You should have given me your powers a long time ago."

"Don't, mum… please!" I cry out and Red shoves the barrel of the gun hard into my temple.

Bang!

Bernice whipped out a gun so fast I didn't even see it until she aimed and fired.

Elizabeth screams. She falls to the glass strewn floor, clutching her chest.

"No!" A collective cry of protestation. Guns are drawn and now we're all held hostage by crazy women.

Crimson liquid pours out of Elizabeth's chest as she lies on her back. It flows through her fingers.

"She'll bleed out and die, you evil bitch!" I want to go to my mother but I'm rooted to the spot in fear for her life. "Do you all see what she's doing? She's a killer!"

The looks on the faces of the girls holding weapons is one of confusion. I know none of them want to do this. I know they are not like Bernice.

"Kill her."

"No!" My mother protest at Bernice's command to off me. "Take it. Take my so-called powers."

"Mum, no!" I raise my hand just as my mother places her hand against Bernice's palm.

A blue glow erupts between them.

"Yes." Bernice hisses. Her eyes go wide with longing and a grin of deranged euphoria parts her lips. "I can feel it. This is who I'm meant to be. This is the power. This is… is… power…"

A cough. Hesitation replaces Bernice's features. "What are you doing to me?"

Suddenly, Bernice tries to pull away. But she

can't. Her hand is melded to my mother's.

I watch as my mum's eyes go wide in confusion. "What have you done, Berenice?"

The woman can't speak. Her throat is being choked from within. "No!" She finally finds her words. "I thought the blood transfusions would work!"

"You put my blood into your own veins?"

Bernice is shaking all over know. She can no longer stand and goes down onto her knees. Still their palms are locked and something happens to the blue glow that connects the two.

It turns red and wet.

Blood.

It's seeping between their fingers.

No one moves. No one says a word. We can't. We are all too stunned to react.

"Help me, you idiots." Bernice calls out to the rejuvenated girls, but none dare to go to her rescue.

Blood oozes, the glowing light goes out. More blood appears and soon enough Bernice is covered in it.

She's bleeding from every pore.

Mum's hand is suddenly released from hers. She pulls away and nearly falls, but rights herself and is steady on her feet.

Everyone watches as Bernice lies on the floor covered in blood. No more words escape her lips. Nothing but a low gurgle issues forth from her throat. Her eyeballs are the only things not crimson with blood, and they remain white, open and staring wide into the eternal void of death.

CHAPTER TWENTY-FOUR

I'm alone in the woods.

Walking over a well-worn trail I pass by birch tree after birch tree until I come to many with carvings in their white trunks.

Each etching reads names and dates that stand out dark grey against the white of the birch tree bark.

I know I'm near the lake of rejuvenation. Each carving is where women have dated their transformations to becoming young again, before or after sleeping under the water. There's a long gap in date etchings before I start to see new carvings.

Women are now returning to the lake to rejuvenate naturally. Bernice is long gone and so are her laboratory ways. It's been a year since the awful events at the compound, but each of us parted ways amicably. With no one to look to as leader, none of the women who held us at gunpoint were willing to fight for her any longer.

"Are you all right?" Colin approaches.

I smile up at him as he nears and kisses me on the cheek. I go into his arms for a warm embrace. It's been a year since the disaster at the compound and already my memories of the place are fading. I don't want to take them with me, should I decided to rejuvenate again, but I don't think I have a choice and only time will tell.

"Have you seen these?" I show Colin the etchings. "The women, they're all coming back to the lake now."

"Your mother has had quite the impact on the natural way of things."

She sure as hell did. My mum took over from Bernice when the evil woman died, but she's helped countless women like us in natural ways. The way of the woods and the lake.

"More women are choosing to rejuvenate in the lake." I run my fingers over a new marking on a tree. The date is from only a week prior. Soon enough the underground tanks will probably be removed entirely. As it stands though, there are still some women who prefer to rejuvenate in a controlled environment. Like when a mother-to-be has a baby at hospital for safety and re-assurance.

While I touch the bark of the tree, Colin moves his hands over my swollen belly.

I'm feeling warm, but not overly heated. I've got on a t-shirt that's stretched over my womb and I'm wearing dark blue maternity jeans.

My womb. My real womb. A swollen tummy that holds a real baby inside.

Mine and Colin's baby. I'm pregnant for real.

ABOUT THE AUTHOR

Suz Korb is a British/American multi-genre author. The Girl in the Woods is her first foray into writing science fiction, the first of more to come. Suz also writes young adult fiction and romantic comedy. For upcoming books and new genres from Suz Korb visit her website: suzkorb.com

OTHER BOOKS BY SUZ KORB

They Keystone

Superstellar

Divine

Trouble in Paradise

Romantic Comedy Shorts

Matrimony Malfunction

Girl Gone Global

Bedevilled

Eve Eden vs. the Zombie Horde

Eve Eden vs. the Blood Sucking Vampires

Eve Eden vs. the Devilish Demon

Printed in Great Britain
by Amazon